PASSIO

Stella had made the mistake of falling in love with Kit Barlow when all he wanted was a casual fling. Once bitten, twice shy. So why did she find herself hankering after Kit when they met again in the Caribbean where it had all started?

PASSIONATE CHOICE

BY

FLORA KIDD

MILLS & BOON LIMITED
15–16 BROOK'S MEWS
LONDON W1A 1DR

First published in Great Britain 1986 by Mills & Boon Limited

© Flora Kidd 1986

Australian copyright 1986 Philippine copyright 1986 This edition 1986

ISBN 0 263 75492 8

Set in Monophoto Times 11 on 11 pt. 01-1086 – 53827

Typeset in Great Britain by Richard Clay (The Chaucer Press) Ltd, Bungay, Suffolk Printed and bound in Great Britain by Collins, Glasgow

CHAPTER ONE

THE swish of curtains being swept aside, the sibilant whisper of waves washing a sandy shore, the sigh of wind among the fronds of palm trees wakened Stella Grayson from a deep sleep and she opened her eyes to see, through the clear glass of a wide patio window, the pattern of palm leaves moving gently against a sky of brilliant sunlit blue.

A voice spoke near by. 'Good morning, Stella.' The voice was female, cheerful and loud. 'I've brought you a breakfast tray, just some coffee, home-made rolls and real English marmalade. The dive-ship has arrived. Brian is up already and having breakfast with the skipper and hopes you'll join him as soon as you've eaten and dressed.'

'Oh. What time is it?' gasped Stella sitting up quickly, pushing her shoulder-length, dark-brown hair behind her shoulders.

'Half-past nine,' replied Harriet Lundgren, owner and manager of the Pelican's Roost Club, an exclusive, remote vacation resort situated on a long tongue of land on the south-west coast of the tropical island of Sanada, the smallest and most far-flung of a chain of islands scattered like a handful of green jewels across the north-eastern part of the Caribbean Sea.

'Good heavens,' exclaimed Stella, 'I intended to be up earlier than this.'

'I expect you needed the sleep after your long journey from London to here,' Harriet said consolingly. A small but well-built woman, with blonde hair cut severely short, her square-jawed face evenly tanned to a golden brown, as were her arms and legs, she was wearing a loose dress made from thin voile-like cotton that hung from straps curving over her shoulders. As she approached the bedside table she smiled brightly showing big white teeth and her smallish grey eyes crinkled at the corners. 'Shall I pour your coffee?' she asked, and without waiting for an answer lifted the coffee-pot from the tray.

'Thank you,' said Stella. 'It's very kind of you to bring my breakfast. I'm sure you have quite enough to do.'

'Not so much this time of the year,' said Harriet in a confidential way. 'In April the bookings fall off and at the end of the month I close up the resort and go north to the States, searching for cooler weather. I have a cottage up in Vermont, by a lake, miles away from the sea, quite different from this. It's because the resort is almost deserted that I asked Brian to come and stay now. Also, it's the best time for diving. There is less wind and the water is very clear. Do you take cream and sugar?'

'No, thanks. I take it black,' replied Stella, sitting up further. 'But you mustn't wait on me. Please tell Brian I'll join him in about fifteen minutes. I'm glad the dive-ship has arrived today. Maybe we'll be able to go diving this afternoon. I expect you were pleased to see Jack Cowan.'

'He hasn't come,' said Harriet with a grimace. 'It seems he's got the flu, so he sent a friend of his to skipper the dive-ship for the first week of your stay, until he's recovered. He didn't want you to be delayed.'

'Well, that was very considerate of him. Brian and I have only three weeks' holiday available,' said Stella.

'Yes, I guess it was considerate of Jack. But it won't be the same without him,' said Harriet walking towards the door of the room. Hand on the doorknob she looked back at Stella and added in a softer, almost sad, voice, 'Jack and my late husband, Larry, were close, very close. Larry thought the world of Jack as a diver and had planned to invite him to come and explore the site of the wreck with him this year, so it won't be quite the same having a complete stranger in charge of the diving. In fact, I'm not at all sure I want any stangers knowing about "our wreck" as I like to call it.'

'I'm a stranger,' Stella pointed out and sipped some coffee.

'Yes, but you're with Brian, as his assistant, so he tells me. And Brian was a great favourite of Larry's too and has known about the wreck ever since Larry found it. But I mustn't stay to talk any longer because you'll be wanting to shower and dress. You have everything you need? Nothing missing from the bathroom?' Leaving the door, Harriet bustled into the small bathroom to check and came out again. 'Sometimes the girl who cleans—her name is Mabel—forgets to put in the clean towels. But I see there are plenty there.' She smiled again and opened the door. 'See you in a few minutes, then, in the dining-room.'

The door closed behind Harriet and Stella leaned back against the pillows stretching her legs under the cotton sheet and smiling a little to herself as she gazed with pleasure at the pattern of palms against the blue sky. The contrast between what she could see and what she usually saw when she woke up in the bedroom of her flat in the city where she lived and worked in England was quite shocking, she thought. Here was brilliance of light and vivid colour. Back home there would be greyness, possibly brought by rain.

But time was going on and Brian—Professor Brian Haines, head of the department of archaeology at Sealand University to whom she was now engaged to be married and for whom she had worked as an assistant lecturer in the department while studying for her master's degree in archaeology for the past two years—would be getting impatient, wondering why she hadn't put in an appearance. She leapt from the bed, ran into the bathroom, showered quickly, and dressed in a thin blue and white shirt belted with a wide white belt over narrow calf-length white 'pirate' trousers. She brushed her silky hair, applied the minimum of make-up to her ivory-skinned, oval-shaped face and regarded her appearance in the mirror seriously with critical dark brown, black-lashed eyes. Then, satisfied with what she could see, she picked up a small white leather shoulder-bag and left the bedroom by the front door, stepping out on to a shady veranda that ran the full width of the one-storey building, a whitewashed stone unit containing, she had been told, six bedroom suites. Another unit about a hundred yards away also contained six bedrooms. Together the two buildings made up the sleeping accommodation at the resort.

Through a plantation of palms, casuarina trees and exotic flowering shrubs she walked along a path that led to a flight of steps going up to the wide terrace of the main resort building. As she mounted the steps she glanced to the left, to the wide horseshoe bay of glittering blue water. Tied up at the end of a jetty belonging to the club was a sleek grey and white ship: the dive-ship carrying all the equipment necessary for scuba diving and for exploring underwater wrecks.

'This way. Come in this way, Stella.' Harriet spoke behind her and Stella turned to find the woman standing in the opening of one of the wide glass doorways that formed part of the outer wall of the main building.

She followed Harriet into a long wide room with a vaulted ceiling. At one end of the room was a bar and at the other a dining area with tables and chairs and doorways leading into the kitchen area. Between the bar and the dining area was a lounge furnished with comfortable sofas and armchairs and occasional tables. Sitting on one of the sofas were Brian and another man, both of them leaning over a coffee-table on which a chart had been spread.

'Here's Stella now,' announced Harriet, since neither of the men seemed to be aware of her or Stella. Immediately Brian looked up and sprang to his feet. Slim and slight, wearing blue shorts and a rather wild sports shirt made from brightly coloured cotton he greeted Stella cheerfully.

'I hope you slept well,' he said.

'Extremely well,' she replied, smiling at him and offering her cheek to his kiss. 'Sorry I'm late.'

'Not to worry, not to worry. We hadn't started to discuss anything.' He slipped a hand through the crook of her arm and urged her towards the coffee-table. 'Come and meet Kit Barlow, acting skipper of the dive-ship. Kit, I'd like you to meet Stella Grayson, my assistant.'

The man who was still leaning over the coffee-table straightened up and rose to his feet in an easy, lithe movement and looked directly at Stella

who, at the mention of his name, had stopped
dead in her tracks, her breath catching sharply in
her throat, hot blood rushing into her normally
pale cheeks then draining away as fast, leaving her
face feeling tight and drawn as shocked surprise
held her rooted to the spot in spite of Brian's
urging hand.

'Hello, Stella.' Kit Barlow's voice was lazy and
deep, lilting with a Southern accent. Under slanted
eyebrows his eyes glinted ice blue through thick
bronze-coloured lashes, while shafts of sunlight
found streaks of gold in his close-cropped curls,
which were of the same bronze hue as his lashes. A
white shirt open to the waist was taut across his
wide shoulders and his brief khaki shorts, belted at
the waist revealed the muscular shapeliness of his
long legs.

'Good morning, Mr Barlow,' Stella replied,
pleased that her voice was cool and steady,
betraying nothing of the shock she had felt on
meeting him again so suddenly three and a half
years after they had parted. She was relieved to see
he took the hint, the slight smile that had begun to
curl his lips and the glow just warming his eyes
both fading. He wasn't going to reveal that he and
she had been previously acquainted.

'It's such a pity Jack has the flu,' Harriet said as
they all sat down, Brian and Stella together on one
sofa, Harriet and Kit on another on the opposite
side of the coffee-table. 'Larry thought so highly of
him and, then, he has had so much experience of
diving and exploring wrecks and searching for
sunken treasure among the islands. Have you done
any underwater exploration before, Mr Barlow?'

'Yes, I have.' A ripple of amusement disturbed
the deep, even flow of his voice. 'Diving has been

my business too, Mrs Lundgren, and I have a
degree in oceanography from the University of
Miami. But if you're at all sceptical of my abilities
both as a diver and skipper of a dive-ship why
don't you call Jack, when you can, and ask him?'

'I'm sure that won't be necessary,' Brian said
hastily, leaning forward. He pushed an envelope
towards Harriet. 'That's the letter of re-
commendation Jack has sent. You'll see he writes
very highly of Kit's abilities.' He glanced at Kit.
'How many have you in your crew?'

'Another diver besides myself and an engineer-
maintenance man for the equipment,' said Kit.

Stella didn't listen to Brian's reply. She was
aware that he was speaking but not of what he was
actually saying. She was too busy looking at the
man who sat opposite her, eyeing him surreptiti-
ously from under her lashes.

Kit hadn't changed much. Perhaps the lines
about his mouth and across his broad forehead
were more incisively carved, perhaps the curve to
his well-shaped lips held a touch of cynicism, but
there was no grey in his tawny hair and his figure
was as lithe and lean as it had been when she had
first known him. In fact, at thirty-five he was more
compellingly attractive to her than he had been at
the age of thirty-one and he certainly didn't look
as if he had spent the last three and a half years
regretting the break-up of their brief but passionate
affair. Handsome, coolly self-confident, his skin
freshly tanned to a becoming golden-brown he
seemed to glow with health and vitality, over-
shadowing completely the other man sitting beside
her.

Her glance slide sideways to Brian who was still
talking. His long, clever face was still pale after a

winter spent in England, and his black, grey-
streaked hair was awry sticking out in all
directions as a result of the habit he had of
running his fingers through it when he was talking
or lecturing. She had known him nearly three and
a half years, ever since she had parted from Kit
and returned to England to continue her studies in
archaeology, and she had learned to like and
respect him. He and she had much in common
including an interest in archaeology and so, when
he had proposed marriage to her a few days ago,
just before they had left England to come to
Sanada she had had no hesitation in accepting.

'Seems quite simple to me.'

The deep, slightly drawling voice was Kit's. Her
glance swerved back to him. Across the table his
eyes met hers. A slight smile warmed their blue
iciness. A dent appeared in his right cheek as his
lips quirked. She looked away from him quickly,
aware again of her colour changing.

'I'd suggest you and Stella dive every morning
and afternoon while the weather is calm,' he was
saying. 'If you need help Gerry or I will come with
you.' He paused, frowning slightly. 'It's as well
you've decided to explore this spring. Another
hurricane like the one that swept through the
islands last November will probably knock the
wreck of that freighter, which is lying across the
crevasse where the remains of the Spanish galleon
are supposed to be, right off the ledges of coral on
which it was wrecked. The sea surge about that
reef in a storm is more than rough and probably
caused the wrecks in the first place.'

'But how do you know?' exclaimed Harriet. 'No
one has dived there since Larry dived last year.'

'I went down with Gerry yesterday afternoon.

We anchored in the cove for the night and came on here this morning,' Kit replied.

'But you had no right,' Harriet almost shouted. 'Only myself and Brian have exploration rights to that reef. We have permission from the chief minister of the islands to explore and search under the freighter for the wreck of the *Santiago*. You had no right to go exploring there yesterday. No right at all.' Bosom heaving, cheeks scarlet, Harriet was obviously furious, but Stella couldn't help wondering if the bluster was to cover fear. The fear that Kit might have seen something Harriet didn't want him to see?

'I didn't say we explored, ma'am,' said Kit patiently. 'All we did was to have a look at the position of the freighter as Jack suggested we did first, to make sure that it was safe for Professor Haines and his assistant to dive under it. You did hire us as consultants, you know.'

'I still don't think you had any right to dive down without Brian being with you,' said Harriet huffily. 'I'm sure Jack would have come here first and would have asked my permission before diving.'

'Mr Barlow was only concerned about our safety, Harriet,' put in Brian diplomatically.

'That's right. I wasn't looking for, or hoping to find, treasure and make off with it,' drawled Kit, his lips curling sardonically. 'Is that what is worrying you, Mrs Lundgren?' he added provocatively.

'No. No. Of course not,' Harriet denied hastily. 'I just want to make it clear to you and your crew that you have no rights to anything that might be found in the way of Spanish artefacts. Both wrecks are registered with Professor Haines's university museum and anything found will be taken there for inspection and cataloguing.'

'There won't be any treasure,' said Brian thoughtfully. 'If it is the ship we think it is, the *Santiago*, it had already been looted by a British privateer, that was lurking in this bay, and was deliberately scuttled and sunk off the reef. The privateer's name, you might be interested to know, was Barlow, Nathaniel Barlow. An ancestor of yours?'

'Probably,' said Kit with a grin. 'Would you and Stella like to go and have a look at the wreck site now? It's a great day for diving. Clear skies and hardly any wind.'

'An excellent idea,' said Brian enthusiastically. 'What do you think, Stella?'

'I can hardly wait to get down there,' she replied. 'Are you coming with us, Harriet?'

'Well, I don't dive, but I would like to go aboard the dive-ship and go out to the reef,' said Harriet. 'You're sure you won't mind having me on board the ship, Mr Barlow?'

'You'll be most welcome, Mrs Lundgren,' he said smoothly and it seemed as if the hostility that had flared so briefly between them was over.

Half an hour later Stella stood on the foredeck of the dive-ship which was called *Sea Urchin* and leaned over the protective rail watching the bow-wave sparkle in the bright sunlight. When they had come aboard the ship Kit had kept aloof from her while he had shown them around, pointing out the rows of yellow and grey scuba tanks, the compressor for filling them with air, and intro-ducing them to Gerry and Matt, the crew. Now he was with Brian in the wheelhouse, steering the ship out of the bay.

She was glad he was ignoring her, she told herself, because she didn't want either Brian or Harriet to know that she and Kit had met before. Once they knew there would be too many questions asked, questions she would find difficult to answer without betraying that her relationship with Kit had once been intimate—for almost nine months. Her lips curled wryly as she recalled how intimate they had been, as intimate and as close as a woman and a man could get. Lovers, they had been, without the commitment of marriage.

'Oh, here you are,' Harriet said beside her in a slightly out-of-breath voice. 'Isn't this exciting to be actually going out to the reef? I wish I could see the wreck of the freighter. Really see it, I mean. Of course, I've studied the photographs Larry took of it, but that isn't the same as seeing it and being able to get under it to see the remains of the other wreck. I'm really quite envious of you because you're going to dive down to it.'

'You should learn to dive,' murmured Stella.

'I did try once but couldn't get down more than two fathoms. Sinus trouble,' replied Harriet. 'So I'm afraid I'll have to do the exploring under the freighter vicariously, live it through your and Brian's experience. You must tell me about everything you do underwater and about what you see and find. Will you?'

'Of course. I'll be glad to.'

'I still can't help wishing that Jack Cowan was with us,' sighed Harriet. 'I'd feel much happier, more confident if he were here.'

'Perhaps he'll come when he's recovered from the flu,' Stella said.

'I hope so. Have you met this Kit Barlow before?'

The question coming abruptly as it did startled Stella. She glanced quickly at the other woman. Harriet, leaning on the rail beside her, was watching her with narrowed, shrewd grey eyes.

'No. What makes you think I have?' she retorted quickly.

'You seemed more than a little surprised when Brian introduced him to you.'

'I was surprised.' Stella was cautious. Harriet was more observant than she appeared. Under that breezy friendly manner she was hiding a sharp curiosity about other people. 'You see I was expecting Jack Cowan. I was a little disappointed too, I think. You had told me so much about Jack last night and I was looking forward to meeting him.'

'I see,' Harriet nodded and looked down at the swishing, sparkling water. 'I guess you've never been in the islands before or anywhere in the Caribbean area.'

'I visited the Bahamas a few years ago,' replied Stella warily. 'I have a friend who lives in Nassau, Shirley Masters. We studied history together at university. She married a Bahamian, Josh Masters, who was studying medicine. He's practising as a doctor in Nassau now and I stayed with them for the Christmas holidays about four years ago and took some diving lessons.'

'Really? Kit Barlow is from Nassau, at least that's what it says in the letter Jack sent. Kit is short for Christopher, isn't it?'

'Yes. I believe so.'

'I wonder, I just wonder if he's a son of Walter Barlow,' mused Harriet, still gazing at the bow-wave.

'Who is Walter Barlow?'

'Oh, you wouldn't have heard of him, I don't suppose,' said Harriet. 'He is, or rather he was, he died two years ago, the owner of a small shipping-line freighting goods between the States and the Caribbean Islands. He used to spend a lot of time on New Providence Island. Had a big villa near Nassau. Was married to a British woman whom he met there. He left millions when he died, I hear.'

A big house near Nassau. Stella had a sudden flash of memory, of a huge room filled with people, wide windows opening on to a terrace and beyond the terrace, a beach glimmering in the moonlight and the sea lapping the sand. She had looked across the room and right into the vivid blue eyes of a stranger who had been staring at her.

'How do you know so much about this Walter Barlow?' she asked, trying to appear casual.

'He was from the same neck of the woods as I am. From Charleston, South Carolina. There have always been close trade connections between the Carolinas and the Bahamas, you know and the Barlow shipping-line goes way back, to the time before the War of Independence.'

'Oh,' said Stella limply.

'But if Kit Barlow is one of those Barlows, what is he doing here skippering a dive-ship instead of Jack Cowan?' Harriet continued with her musing.

'I don't know,' said Stella weakly. 'You could always ask him.'

Harriet turned her head and flashed one of her brilliant smiles.

'I intend to,' she said firmly. 'I intend to find out everything about him as soon as I can. Oh, look,' she added as the ship's engines slowed. 'We're nearly at the reef. How calm it looks for once. I guess you're going to find conditions perfect for diving today.'

The *Sea Urchin* was anchored in a small bay close to the reef of coral that ran out from the south-western headland of the island. Stella and Brian as well as Kit and Gerry made preparations to dive, fitting on tanks and weight-belts, flippers and masks before stepping off the ladder into the warm silken water.

Floating downwards slowly Stella followed the other divers to the rusting hulk of a small freighter which was lying on two outgrowths of coral across a sort of gully, a dark space in and out of which shoals of silvery and coloured fish swam.

She felt a touch on her arm and turned. Kit was beside her, long and lean and tanned, wearing only swimming trunks, his face covered by the scuba mask. He pointed to the entrance to the gully under the freighter and indicated that she should follow him. She nodded and breathing deeply of the air in her tank let herself drift down deeper, following him as she had followed him so many times when they had gone diving together, trusting implicitly in his competence and experience as a diver.

It was dark under the freighter and torches were needed. Brian was already there with Gerry. When he saw her he took her by the hand and showed her the few timbers lying almost buried under the sand: the unmistakable relics of what had once been a wooden ship.

At the end of half an hour, the length of time the air in their tanks lasted, they all made for the surface and the bright, hot sunshine. Harriet was waiting for them on the afterdeck and, as soon as he had shed his diving gear, she accosted Kit going with him up the steps to the wheelhouse. Gerry, a cheery-faced young man of about twenty-four who had long blond hair and a New York accent, showed Stella to a cabin in which she could change out of her wet swimsuit and into her other clothes. When she was dry and dressed she left the cabin and made her way again to the foredeck. Looking back and up at the wheelhouse as the ship was steered slowly away from the reef she noted that Harriet was still with Kit, talking to him as he steered, asking him questions, no doubt, about his family and possibly asking him also if he had ever met herself before. Stella could only hope that he would be as reticent about himself with Harriet as he had always been with her.

'So what do you think of Barlow?' asked Brian coming to join her at the rail.

'Think of him?' she exclaimed. The question surprised her. She had expected Brian to ask her what she thought of the wrecks they had seen. 'What do you mean? Why should I think anything about him?'

'I just wondered what your opinion of him was after that little fracas between him and Harriet this morning. I thought he was rather insolent.'

'He seems to be making up for his insolence now,' Stella replied, glancing again up at the wheelhouse. Harriet appeared to be steering the ship under Kit's supervision. 'I think he was being very honest this morning. He has . . .' She broke off quickly realising that she had been about to betray to Brian that she knew more about Kit than would have been possible after having only just made his acquaintance. She had been going to tell Brian that Kit had a reputation for speaking his mind directly and often forcefully. 'I mean,' she went on quickly, 'he seems to be straightforward and knowledgeable.'

'I hope you're right about him making up for his insolence to Harriet. In spite of the way she speaks and behaves she is very sensitive, especially about Larry's reputation as an underwater archaeologist. I hope we'll be able to prove that the earlier wreck was a Spanish galleon called the *Santiago* as Larry guessed it is. She will be mortified if he was wrong. She's spending a lot of money on this little private expedition of ours.'

'All to vindicate Professor Lundgren's reputation,' murmured Stella. 'She must have been very fond of him.'

'It was a second marriage for both of them. Her first husband was an extremely wealthy man. He bought land on this island and developed the Pelican Roost resort club for his wealthy friends to stay in. He was much older than she, apparently, and when he died he left everything to her.'

'Professor Lundgren must have been a lot older than her too,' said Stella thoughtfully, remembering the silvery-haired American archaeologist who had visited Brian only a year ago to talk about the *Santiago*, just before he had been killed quite tragically in a car crash. 'She must be about forty and he was sixty-six. Old enough to be her father.'

'People might say that about you and me, when we marry,' said Brian quietly. 'Will you mind?'

'I'll try not to,' she replied lightly, uncomfortably recalling the taunt made by her sister, Audrey, when she had told her of her acceptance of Brian's proposal. But he's old enough to be your father. He must be forty-five or more. And he's been divorced, hasn't he? Wasn't there a story going about that his ex-wife divorced him on the grounds of mental cruelty? Stella had then defended Brian and had told Audrey that his ex-wife hadn't appreciated his fine mind and his scholarly pursuits in the way that she did herself but Audrey had given her a mocking glance and remarked: Oh, in that case you and he are well matched. You won't object when he goes off to poke about old ruins and wrecks instead of making love to you. You won't mind because you're so cold and passionless yourself.

'I can't help wondering though, Stella, why no other man has snatched you up and married you,' Brian's murmuring voice broke into her thoughts. 'There must have been others who have been attracted to you.'

He was probing, delicately it was true, into her past and she wondered whether now was the time to admit to him that she had met Kit Barlow over four years ago in Nassau and had fallen in love with him so deeply that for nine months she had pushed aside her ambition to become an archaeologist and had lived with him on his sailing yacht *Siren*, cruising about the islands of the Caribbean.

'Supposing there was someone,' she said slowly. 'Supposing I'd had a lover and had lived with him for a while. What would you think? Would you still want to marry me?'

'A hypothetical question?' he queried, somewhat amused. 'I can't believe you would ever do something like that. You're too reserved, too intellectual, too wholesome . . .'

'Oh, Brian,' she interrupted him laughingly. 'You make me sound like a heroine out of a Jane

Austen novel. But I'm not. I'm real. I'm a real woman with blood in my veins, with longings and desires as well as ambitions. Now, tell me, if you knew that I had lived with another man for nearly a year without being married to him what would you think?'

The engines were slowing again and the ship was turning towards the jetty. The beach belonging to the resort shimmered white in the sunlight and behind it the dusty green palms and casuarinas cast deep dark shadows around the plain white buildings.

'Ah, we're nearly there,' said Brian.

'You haven't answered my question,' Stella reminded him.

He frowned at her, rubbing the top of the rail with both hands uncertainly.

'Stella, why . . .?' he began but she interrupted him again.

'Please, Brian. Give me an answer,' she pleaded.

'All right.' He heaved a sigh. 'I'll answer it. I wouldn't understand how you of all women could behave in such a way. That's my answer.'

'So it would make a difference to how you feel about me?'

'Yes. It would, a great difference,' he snapped and turning away from her he strode to the ladder that went up to the wheelhouse and began to climb it.

CHAPTER TWO

DINNER that evening was served as usual at the resort, buffet-style in the dining-room. Stella was helping herself from the array of food—local lobster, barbecued chicken, rice and peas, spicy beans, crisp salad, hot home-made rolls and soft butter when Harriet came bustling through a swing door from the kitchen. The woman gave a quick glance at Brian, who was in conversation with some other guests who were staying at the resort, a party of sport fishermen who had flown in from St Thomas by charter place to try the fishing on Sanada Bank, then stood close to Stella and whispered, 'I asked him and I was right. He is related to Walter Barlow. He's the younger son and is now in the business, the freighting business I mean, with his elder brother. Right now he's on vacation cruising about on his yacht. That's how he ran into Jack Cowan and offered to bring the ship here until Jack is well enough to come.' Harriet gave a little chuckle as she rearranged the dishes on the long buffet table. 'He is rather attractive. Do you think five years in our ages would be too much for me to have a satisfactory relationship with him?'

Stella turned to her, her mouth opening in amazement.

'You mean . . .' she began.

'Oh, I'm always on the look-out for an attractive man to have an affair with,' said Harriet with a chuckle. 'But I have to admit this is the first time I've ever considered a man younger than myself. And he does have an added attraction. He's wealthy. Larry wasn't.' Her face sobered, lines hardening discontentedly. 'And this place is losing money. I've got to find someone who'll buy some shares in it or I'll go bankrupt. That's why ...' She smiled again. 'But I'm rattling on too much and you're wanting to have your dinner. Do take as much as you want. Virginia, the cook, always makes too much.' She glanced again at the party of men. 'Kit said he and the crew will come over later to join us for drinks. They preferred to eat on board tonight although I told them they could eat here for free.'

'You're too generous,' murmured Stella. 'That's why you'll go bankrupt.'

'You can say that again,' said Harriet with another laugh and whisked, with a flurry of her long, loose, multi-coloured gown, back into the kitchen.

Somehow, Stella thought as she was eating, only half listening to the conversation that was going on between Brian and the Americans, somehow she had to intercept Kit on his way out for drinks. She had to see him alone to prevent him from telling Harriet that he had met her in Nassau a few years ago. Once Harriet knew, Brian would know and once Brian knew the questions would come; questions she would prefer not to answer about an affair Brian would never understand.

It would be best if she made some excuse, left the dining-room and went down to the dive-ship to see Kit before he left it to come up here. The problem was thinking up an excuse. She supposed the usual one would have to do, so when Brian offered to get her some coffee and some fresh coconut pie for dessert she declined and said, 'I'm afraid I have a headache. I think I'll go to my room, take a couple of aspirins and lie down. I want to be really fit if we're going diving tomorrow.' She pushed back her chair and stood up. He stood up too, looking anxious.

'I'll walk with you to your room,' he said.

'No. No. Please stay here, have your coffee and pie. Harriet says the crew off the dive-ship are coming to have drinks so you stay and be here when they come.'

'You're quite sure?'

'Quite sure. I'm sorry to be such a wet blanket but it's best if I go to lie down so that I'll be in good trim tomorrow. Good night.'

'Good night, then, dear,' he said, kissing her cheek, and she made her escape quickly just as Harriet came bustling out of the kitchen again.

The moon had risen and everything was silvered by its radiance. Under the leaning coconut palms shadows were thick and black. At first, she followed the pathway which led to the block of rooms in which hers was located, just in case anyone was watching her, but before she reached the building she altered course and struck off along another path which led down to the beach and the jetty at the end of which the dive-ship was tied up, light glimmering from its wheelhouse.

Along the jetty she walked quickly and up the gangway to step on to the side deck of the ship. The doorway to the main cabin was closed but she was able to slide it open and step inside. A single light glowing from a bulkhead showed her that the cabin was empty so she left and walked along the deck to the companionway which led down to the lower deck and the small sleeping cabins. At the

bottom of the companionway she paused to listen.
The only noise she could hear was the creaking of
a warp that tied the ship to the jetty.

'Hello,' she called out. 'Anyone on board?'

There was no answer so after knocking on the
doors of the small cabins and opening them to
look in only to find each room untenanted, she
went back to the main deck, realising with a rueful
dismay that Kit and his crew had already left the
ship and gone in to the resort. They must have
been on their way through the plantation of trees
and shrubs when she had been pretending to go to
her bedroom by another path.

Slowly she walked back along the jetty. There
was no point in going back to the dining-room or
to the bar and lounge. She couldn't talk to Kit
confidentially in front of Brian and both Harriet
and Brian would be surprised if she returned. He
would never believe that her headache had gone so
quickly.

She stepped off the jetty on the beach which
curved away to her left, the pale sand shimmering
under the moon. A slight breeze had sprung up
rustling the palm fonds and rippling the dark water,
causing tiny moon-glinting waves to rush up the
beach. Taking off her sandals she walked along the
beach her feet sinking in the soft sand, her head
drooped in thought.

She must see Kit alone before he told Brian or
Harriet that he knew her. Brian wouldn't
understand if he learned that she had spent nine
months with Kit, living with him, loving with him,
sharing laughter and tears, calms and tempests, as
they had sailed about in his yacht. Brian wouldn't
understand, so why tell him?

But if she didn't tell him about her brief but

intensely passionate affair with another man wouldn't she be guilty of deceiving him? Was it really necessary to tell him? Wouldn't it be better to go on pretending she didn't know Kit and had never met him before? But could she depend on Kit?

Had Kit forgotten her? Somehow she didn't think so. How could he have forgotten the hours, the days, the weeks of stolen delight they had experienced together? She had tried to forget but hadn't succeeded. All she had been able to do was to push all memories of love and passion into a secret drawer at the back of her mind; a drawer never to be opened until many years had gone by, until she was safe, and able to open the drawer and flick through the memories without fear of torment, could tear them up and throw them away like so many old photographs of people and places long forgotten.

But this recent unexpected meeting with Kit had forced that drawer open and now the memories were tumbling out unbidden, vivid and heart-stabbing. Most of all that first meeting with him would keep flashing across her mind. Across a crowded room she had looked, seen him and fallen in love with him.

It had been so unlike her to look and love. At the time she had been twenty-two, had not long graduated with an honours degree in history and had already started her studies towards a master's degree in archaeology. Her holiday with her friend, Shirley, in Nassau had been arranged so that she could learn to scuba dive, a skill which would be valuable to her should she wish to participate in any undersea archaeological expeditions.

Ambitious, liberated in her thinking, she had decided at the age of eighteen that romance was not for her and although she had known young men, had worked and studied with them and several had been attracted to her, she had always been the one to set the pace in such affairs, retreating from emotional involvement when an affair had threatened to become serious and interfere with her ambition to have a career, postponing love and passion until she was established in that career, keeping her physical desires damped down and under strict control until such time as she was ready to let them flare up.

And then she had gone to a party in Nassau, had looked across a room at a stranger and from that moment had lost control of her destiny.

Kit hadn't taken long to thread his way through the crowd of talking, laughing party-goers. For a few moments she had been standing alone, Shirley and her husband having been in conversation with another couple. Then, suddenly, Kit had been standing before her, his vivid eyes blazing down at her, his teeth glinting in his slanted smile.

'I'll introduce myself since no one else will,' he had said holding out a big tanned hand. 'I'm Kit Barlow. You are?'

'Stella Grayson.' She had put her hand in his, had felt its warmth and strength.

'From England, I would guess.'

'Yes.'

'On holiday here?'

'Staying with a friend of mine. Shirley Masters. She and Josh, her husband, brought me to this party. Are you . . . do you . . .?' Words had failed her because he had still been gazing at her and holding her hand tightly as if he would never let it go. She had felt a strange excitement throbbing through her and the rest of the people in the room had ceased to exist. She had been blind and deaf to everyone except the tall, golden man who had held her hand. 'This house belongs to someone called Barlow,' she had whispered rather lamely.

'Let's just say I'm a close relative of his,' he had replied softly. 'Shall we take a walk along the beach?'

Still holding her hand he had led her from the room through a french window on to a veranda, down some steps and on to a small private beach, a crescent of yellow sand. In the dark sky a thin silver sickle of a moon had shone, much like the moon that was shining tonight.

There had been no strain between them during that first walk along a beach, no awkwardness. They had talked to each other easily and naturally, no longer strangers, behaving as if they had known each other all their lives, but it was not until she had told him that there was only a week left of her holiday and that she couldn't afford any more diving lessons that he told her that he had been diving professionally for some years and offered to take her down to the islands of the Exumas on his yacht to give her more instruction.

'Have you visited the Exumas?' he had asked.

'No.'

'You should. There is no better diving anywhere. I'll be sailing across to Highbourne Cay day after tomorrow on the start of my "goofing off" vacation. Why not come with me?'

'Goofing off? she had exclaimed, a little confused by his casual invitation to join him. 'What do you mean?'

'Going off and leaving all responsibilities behind, doing what I want to do when I want to do it, pleasing myself for a few months, or a year, or maybe even longer. Haven't you ever wanted to do that? To escape from work, from commitment?'

'No. I can't say I have. I've always had to work so hard to get what I want, studying to win scholarships to pay my way through university and keep up the standard of my marks to get my degree. I've never been able to afford to "goof off" as you call it.'

He had stopped walking then and had swung her round to face him. 'But you can afford to come to the Exumas with me. You have all next week free. I'll show you how to dive, Stella. Every day we'll anchor in a different place. Come with me,' he had whispered.

'Just you and me,' she had said, whispering also, tempted by his suggestion but also fearful of it.

'Just you and me.'

'But ... I have to fly home to England next Friday from here. The university term begins on January 15th and I must be there. A new professor is taking over the department and I'd like to be there to meet him.'

'You're much too serious,' he had murmured, bending towards her. 'Time you learned to loosen up a little, to take life as it comes instead of always planning ahead. Time you "goofed off" and had some fun, Stella-with-stars-in-your-eyes. Time that someone like me came into your life and made love to you ...'

His lips had found hers and she hadn't resisted. Brief yet devastating that first kiss of his had been. It had gone straight to the very heart of her, suggestively inviting her to respond before he had withdrawn. In a breathless silence they had stood looking at each other and then with a gruff laugh he had swept her into his arms and his lips had plundered hers again.

And she had responded, oh, how she had responded. Groaning a little as she relived those magic moments on another beach Stella seemed to feel again the pressure of his lips, the urgent message of his hands caressing her.

She had gone with him to the Exumas intending to fly back to Nassau from Georgetown when the week was over but when the time had come for her to leave she had been very reluctant to go ashore to catch the plane.

'You don't have to go, if you don't want to,' Kit had said to her. 'You could stay on, sail with me through the islands down to Puerto Rico and the Virgins, on to the Leewards and Windwards. We might even make it to Venezuela. Just nine months I'm going for. Have to be back by the end of next September because there's something else I want to do then. Think of it, Stella.' He had sat down beside her on the berth in the main cabin of the yacht where she had been packing her zipped holdall. Since he had kissed on the beach he hadn't touched her and their relationship for that week had been entirely without physical intimacy. It had been a wonderful, joyous friendship as they had swum and dived together and discussed everything under the sun. But all the time she had been aware of his physical attraction for her and had often had difficulty in keeping her hands off him.

'Think of it,' he had continued, moving closer to her until his breath had wafted her cheek. 'We would take our time, diving when we want, lazing about when we want. There'll be plenty to see underwater to please you, old wrecks we could visit. It would be nine months of stolen delight if you'll come with me.'

'There must be some other woman you could take with you, someone you know better than you know me,' she had said shakily, refusing to look at him because to have done so would have destroyed her opposition to his suggestion completely.

'There are other women but none I like better than you. And, anyway, it would be part of the delight of getting to know each other better. Come with me, Stella. Stay with me.'

'But . . . my studies at university . . .'

'You'll be studying,' he said with a soft laugh. 'You'll be learning how to dive really well. And those other studies, that university of yours will still be there next September. But I won't be here. And this chance you have to "goof off" won't come again.'

'I . . .' she had begun turning to him and that had been her undoing. The expression which had been blazing in his eyes had conveyed a message no woman could have misinterpreted. 'I'll miss the plane to Nassau,' she had whispered, making one last effort to resist him.

'You're not going to catch it if I refuse to row you ashore.'

'You wouldn't do that.'

'Oh, wouldn't I?' he had jeered. 'You know you don't want to catch it. You know you want to stay.'

'But if I do stay and go with you what will everyone think?'

'Everyone. Who the hell is everyone?' he had demanded.

'My parents, the university authorities, Shirley . . .'

'And I believed you to be adult; a grown up liberated woman,' he had taunted. 'Do you really care what they will think?'

'Yes, I do.'

'Then you're very different from me,' he had replied coldly. 'OK. If their opinion is more important to you than doing something you want to do, I'll row you ashore to catch that plane.'

His sudden withdrawal then had been more successful than his attempts to persuade her had been. Realisation that in a few minutes she would be parting from him, never having really known him, had overwhelmed her unexpectedly and she had cried out, 'But I don't want to catch the plane. I want to stay. I want to go with you, sail with you, dive with you, have nine months of . . . of stolen delight. Oh, please don't take me ashore, Kit. I'll come with you and I won't care what anyone says or thinks.'

He had turned back to her then, had taken her in his arms and there had been no more argument and that night for the first time they had shared the double bunk in the forward cabin, sleeping together and making love.

Perhaps it was because they had both known they were not going to be together for ever that they had lived in harmony for those nine months, sharing everything, and yet, now she came to think of it, it was only when their time together was coming to an end that she had begun to feel a strain as she had realised she hadn't wanted to leave Kit, that she had wanted commitment to him and from him.

They had returned to Nassau as he had planned in the last week of September, just before the first hurricane of the season had blown up. Even now she could recall how hot and sultry the weather had been when *Siren* had been steered into its berth at the Nassau Harbour Club marina and the lines had been made fast. Leaving Kit on the dock talking to the dock master she had gone below decks to fix a cold drink for him and for herself and she had been approaching the steps up to the cockpit, a glass in each hand when she had heard a high-pitched, excited female voice calling, 'Kit, Kit. Oh, Kit, darling you're back at last. Tom heard you calling harbour control on the radio and told me you were on your way in so I came straight down to welcome you.'

Standing on the ladder, the glasses still in her hand, her head just above the hatchway, Stella had been able to see without being seen and she had watched a young woman with blonde-streaked hair tied back in a pony-tail, dressed in brief blue shorts revealing long tanned legs fling herself at Kit, wind her arms around his neck and kiss him very thoroughly.

'Oh, Kit,' the young woman had continued in that high voice so that anyone who had wanted to hear could have heard every word ringing out. 'I'm so glad you're back. Now we can get married. Now we can set the date. Oh, it's wonderful to see you.'

Stella had had time to see Kit take the young woman's arms from around his neck and push her away from him all the time laughing.

'It's good to see you too, Sherri,' he had said. He had put an arm about the young woman's shoulders and turning her had guided her along the dock towards the club buildings, away from the *Siren* and away from Stella.

Stunned by what she had just seen and heard

Stella had retreated down the ladder to the cabin. Placing one of the glasses on the galley counter she had sat down in the saloon and had sipped her drink slowly, trying to deal with the feeling of intense disappointment and disillusion that had swept over her and all the time the voice of the woman called Sherri had been ringing through her mind: Now we can get married. Now we can set the date.

When they had embarked on their cruise Kit had told her he would return to Nassau before the end of September because there was something else he wanted to do and that had suited her because she had planned to return to university when the nine months were over. Never once had she thought that the something Kit wanted to do was get married to another woman. Strictly single, he had always described himself, and intending to stay that way for as long as he could, and for a while, having been strictly single herself, she had understood and accepted his views.

But then, at the end of nine months of loving him and living with him, she had longed for him to ask her to marry him. Instead she had heard a woman called Sherri say to him: Now we can get married. She had seen the woman kiss him, and the way he had put his arm around Sherri's shoulders affectionately and realised he had come back to get married.

Alone in the cabin she had sat, numb with misery as she faced up to reality, the reality that for Kit, his nine months with her, those months of enchantment among tropical islands had been nothing more than a last fling before he gave up the freedom of being strictly single.

Eventually her pride had asserted itself and she

had shaken off the misery, reminding herself that she had gone into the affair with her eyes wide open expecting nothing by way of commitment and, at first, not expecting to make any commitment herself. She and Kit had agreed to split when they returned to Nassau so the time had come to split.

When he had come back to the boat he had found her all ready to leave, her bags packed, her shorts and sun-top changed for crisp white cotton pants, an emerald green blouse and a loose, white cotton jacket. She had been lugging one of her bags up from the cabin to the cockpit.

'What are you doing?' he had asked approaching the hatchway with the intention of going down the ladder so that she had been forced to back down.

'Leaving,' she had replied brightly. 'This is the end of the line, isn't it? Would you mind taking this bag?'

He had taken it from her and dropped it on the floor of the cockpit and before she had time to pick up another bag and push it up to him he had run down the ladder.

'You don't have to leave yet,' he had said.

'Oh, I think so,' she had replied. 'It's the best way. I'd like to go ashore and spend a night in a hotel, maybe two, if I can't fly out tomorrow ...'

'You don't have to stay in a hotel. You could stay on board or you could ...'

'No, thank you. I've had enough of living on a yacht. I'd like some comfort, some luxury, a bathroom to myself, some time to get my act together, make some long-distance calls, attend to my hair, book a seat on a flight to London, be by myself for a while before going home,' she had interrupted him sharply.

He had stood looking at her, hands on his hips, his eyes dark and expressionless, his face giving nothing away of how he felt about her decision. If he had spoken then. If he had only said: Stella, don't go. Stay with me, she would have capitulated to his demands completely. But he had said nothing. He couldn't have said anything and the shadow of a young woman called Sherri had moved between them.

'You're really keen to get back to your studies and get that master's degree, aren't you?' he had said at last. 'Nothing else, no one else matters.' One corner of his lip had twisted downwards in a sour grimace. 'OK' he had shrugged and had taken the bag she had been holding from her. 'You could always stay in a room here, at the Nassau Harbour Club,' he had suggested.

'No. I'd prefer a bigger hotel, one nearer the town and the airport.'

'Then I'll go and call a taxi for you,' he had said coolly.

Not much more had been said. The taxi had come and he had helped the driver to put her bags in the boot.

'We won't waste time in a tearful goodbye scene,' he had remarked drily, holding out his right hand to her. 'We had a great time, Stella, and I shan't forget. No regrets, I hope?'

'Oh, no. No regrets.' She had smiled at him even though she had been crying inside.

'Will you write, let me know when you get that degree?'

'No. I don't think so. Goodbye, Kit ... and thanks, thanks for everything.' Her voice had choked and she had almost treated him to the tearful farewell scene. Pulling her hand from his grasp she had stepped blindly into the back of the taxi and closed the door. When the cab moved forward she had turned to wave but Kit hadn't been there. He had gone.

And so it had ended, their short love affair, coolly and without recriminations and she had truly believed that she would never see him again.

Realising that she had reached the end of the beach where a jumble of rocks jutted out into the bay Stella stopped walking and wandered down to the edge of the water. The little waves lapped her bare feet. Across the wide expanse of the bay, lights twinkled from the houses of the village. Behind her, leaves rustled. All was quiet and peaceful. No wonder tired business people came to such places to relax for a week or so and to forget for a while the stresses and strains of city life. And yet, Harriet had told her that if she didn't find someone to invest in the Pelican's Roost it would go bankrupt.

'Thinking of going skinny dipping?' asked a slightly drawling voice behind her. 'I'll keep you company if you like. Best not to swim alone.'

Although her nerves leapt with a sudden warm pleasure at the sound of Kit's voice she turned towards him slowly. He was standing a few feet away from her, a tall, shapely figure, his white shirt gleaming in the moonlight, his face silvered and shadowed.

'You've been following me?' she asked.

'I have.'

'But how did you know I'd come this way?'

'When I realised you weren't going to put in an appearance in the bar I decided to go back to the ship. I saw you step off the jetty and on to the beach.' He stepped towards her until he was very close to her. 'This is some coincidence us meeting again like this,' he said softly.

'Have we met before?' she parried defensively and he laughed, a pleasant infectious sound, a familiar beloved sound.

'How like you to play it cool,' he scoffed. 'You know damned well we've met before.'

'I don't remember,' she said, persisting in her pretence of not knowing him.

'Then perhaps this will remind you,' he retorted, no longer gently mocking, his voice roughened by some disturbance of feeling and taking hold of her shoulders he jerked her forward and kissed her.

She made no attempt to avoid his lips but let their hot hardness press against the cool softness of hers until response flickered into life deep within her, a small flame that blazed up fiercely and suddenly when his arms slid around her and his tongue forced its way between her lips. For a long time they kissed, indulging in the familiar erotic sensations that they were able to arouse in each other until Kit lifted his mouth from hers, bit the lobe of her ear gently and whispered, 'Remember now?'

She stepped away from him, reluctantly withdrawing from the temptation of his embrace, disciplining her excited senses, refusing as always to let him see how he could penetrate to the secret core of her being, take over and dominate the inner passionate person who hid behind the cool façade she presented to the world as a rule.

'Perhaps a vague memory stirs,' she replied coolly. 'About four years ago, wasn't it? In Nassau? We met at a party at a house in Lyford Cay.'

He stood still and silent. The little waves

splashed gently about her feet. The night wind
sighed in the palms. The sickle moon shone down
out of the dark blue tropical sky, and the air was
warm, scented with unseen blossoms. It was a
night for romance, for love, like many of the
nights they had walked together on similar beaches
on other islands. But there was no romance
tonight. She had destroyed any romance there
might have been by speaking coldly and purpose-
fully, thinking of his marriage to Sherri and her
own promise to Brian.

At last Kit moved, folding his arms across his
chest. He said rather harshly, 'Are you trying to
tell me you don't remember the months we lived
together?'

'I . . . I'm trying to tell you that I would prefer
to forget that episode in my life,' she replied. 'I'm
really surprised you remember and I would prefer
it if you forgot about it too. You see,' she drew a
deep breath to control her voice, to prevent it
expressing the turmoil which had stirred up within
her when he had kissed her. 'You see,' she went on
steadily and coolly, 'when this little underwater
expedition is over and we return to England Brian
and I are going to be married.'

CHAPTER THREE

THERE was another silence and again neither of them moved. Then Kit said, slowly and softly with just a suspicion of mockery in his voice, 'So that's the way of it. You, who didn't care much for commitment, as I remember, are going to take the big step and marry the professor for better or worse. How come?'

'What do you mean how come?' she demanded, deciding she had had enough of standing in front of him, her face fully illuminated by the moonlight while his was in the shadows. He could see any expression that flitted across her features while she could see nothing clearly of his. Turning she began to walk back along the beach and he fell into step beside her.

'I mean why. Why are you going to marry him? Has he compromised you? Are you going to have his child?' The mockery was still there in his voice, cruelly taunting. Yet the Kit she had known had never been like this, at least not with her. He had changed after all.

'No. Of course I'm not going to have his baby,' she retorted. 'We haven't ...' She broke off realising that she had been about to confide him as if he and she were close friends who told each other everything. She had been going to tell him that she and Brian were not physically intimate.

'Ah, so you're not lovers yet,' he jeered. 'That figures. He doesn't look as if he has much fire in his belly.'

'How can you say that?' She turned on him angrily. 'You hardly know him.'

'True,' he agreed equably. 'I'm just judging him on what I've seen of him so far. So you haven't told him about our adventure together?'

'No, I haven't.'

'Going to?'

'No.'

'Deliberately deceiving him?'

'I don't think so. If I told him about it he wouldn't understand. He would be upset and hurt so it's best that he doesn't know. What is past is past and is best forgotten, but I have to ask you not to tell him anything about it either. Please, Kit, you won't say anything to him about you and me having met before, will you? Please.'

They had stopped walking and were facing each other again.

'What's my silence on the subject worth to you?' he challenged her, bending towards her so that he could look into her moonlit eyes. 'What bribe do you have to offer to keep me quiet?'

'You used not to be so unkind,' she accused in a low voice, shaken by his cynicism.

'Maybe I learned how to be from you,' he retorted.

'Wh ... what bribe do you suggest I should offer?' she muttered.

'Oh, I was thinking along the lines of you and I having a couple of nights together, on board the dive-ship. I could easily get rid of Gerry and Matt and we could cruise to some of the other islands.' His voice trailed off into silence—suggestively.

Anger such as she had never known before flared up in Stella and before she knew what she was doing she had raised her hand and slapped his face. 'How dare you?' she gasped. 'I would never think of . . . of stooping so low to buy your silence. Just because I . . . I once lived with you and slept with you doesn't give you the right to assume that I'm the sort of woman who . . . who would use her body as a bribe. Never would I do that. Never.'

Turning on her heel she set off along the beach walking fast and furiously, her heart beating madly, her face flushed with anger while tears brimmed in her eyes; tears because Kit whom she had once loved with all her heart and soul could have such a low opinion of her. After a while she became aware that he was loping along beside her.

'OK. I apologise,' he said calmly, then added with a soft laugh, 'you still have a devil of a temper. I haven't been slapped like that since I was a kid. But you don't have to worry about me telling Haines anything about you and me. You should know I'm not the guy to spill my guts about my personal life to an absolute stranger. Or to my friends.' There was a note of rebuke in his voice.

'I know you're like that or at least you were like that, but I had to make sure,' she replied quietly, her anger fading as suddenly as it had flared up. 'And . . . and I'm sorry I slapped you. I hope you haven't said anything to Harriet about us, either.'

'No, I haven't. Why would I?'

'You and she seemed to be very chummy this afternoon and she told me she was going to find out all about you. Then at dinner she said that her guess about you was right, that you are the younger son of someone from her home town, a Walter Barlow. Why didn't you ever tell me it was in your parents' house that we met?'

'It didn't seem important at the time,' he replied carelessly.

'She asked me if you and I had ever met before. She'd noticed my surprise when I saw you this morning.'

'Yes, you did change colour rather violently,' he remarked with a laugh. 'I guess I had the advantage of you there. I knew the name of Professor Haines's assistant. Jack told me the names of the people I would be dealing with and I'd decided there couldn't possibly be two Stella Graysons in the world who were also archaeologists. I take it you got the degree?'

'Yes, I got the degree.'

'Congratulations.'

'And I'm now working towards a doctorate.'

'Under the tutelage of Professor Haines, I've no doubt.'

'Of course.' There was another silence as they walked on slowly, so close to each other that occasionally his bare arm brushed against hers, but even without that slight contact she was tinglingly aware of him and found herself wishing he would take hold of her hand as he used to whenever they had walked together. Then, knowing she would never learn anything about him unless she asked direct questions she said, 'So what are you doing these days? Still free-lancing, offering your services as a diver wherever you see an opportunity?

'When I get the chance,' he replied. 'I joined my brother, Tom, in the business, the shipping and trading business, soon after you and I returned to Nassau. That's what I went back to do. I'd promised the old man—my father—I'd go into the business when he retired and after I'd had a few months of "goofing off".'

'I wish I'd known. I wished you'd told me,' she complained.

'Why? Would it have made a difference to you?'
He sounded surprised.

'Yes, it would. You see, I had the impression all
the time I was with you that you were . . . oh, I
don't know how to put it.'

'You had the impression I was a drifter.
Possibly unreliable and irresponsible. Perhaps a
playboy?' he suggested with a touch of amusement.
They had almost reached the jetty. There seemed
to be more light glinting from the dive-ship,
through the portholes on the lower deck. They
stopped walking as if mutually agreeing that this
was the place where they must part and turned to
each other.

'I was all of those for a while,' Kit continued,
still amused. 'I had a great time. And it's normal,
isn't it, in the development of a man for him to
play about, look around in his youth? If he doesn't
do it, he tends to hanker to do it later in life. He
doesn't settle down.'

'And are you settled now?'

He appeared to give her question some thought,
looking away from her at the moonlit water, then
down again at her shadowed face.

'No. I can't say I am,' he said slowly. 'I still
"goof off" when I can.' He paused then added,
'Like now.'

'Have you left the company?'

'No. Just taken some leave of absence to cruise
about for a while.'

'In *Siren*?'

'No. Another yacht. A bigger one. Thirty-seven
feet.'

'A sloop?' she queried, interested in spite of her
resolve to keep aloof from him.

'No. A cutter. I took delivery of her a month

ago and decided to take time off for a shake-down
cruise through the islands. Made it as far as St
Thomas.'

'Alone?'

'No.' The answer was short, repelling any further
questions on that subject. 'In St Thomas I ran into
some diving friends and one of them told me Jack
Cowan had this commission to help with an
underwater exploration off the Sanada reef. I went
to see him and found him lying near to death with flu
and about to get in touch with Harriet Lundgren to
tell her he couldn't make it. I offered to take his place
until he'd recovered. As things are with him he
couldn't really afford to lose the commission.'

'I had no idea you could be so altruistic,' she
mocked.

'No altruism about it,' he replied easily. 'I'm
really interested in what you and Brian Haines are
going to find under the wreck of that freighter.
Harriet Lundgren isn't spending money on hiring
Jack's diving outfit for nothing. Have you any idea
what Larry Lundgren came up with from the site
that made him believe he'd found the wreck of the
Santiago?'

'Some late seventeenth-century artefacts.'

'Such as?'

'Some silver tableware—a plate, a jug, some
forks. Several old coins and, most important of all,
a gold cross set with diamonds and emeralds, the
cross of the Order of Santiago, that could have
only belonged to a wealthy Spanish nobleman.'

'But if the *Santiago* had already been looted by
the pirate surely she wouldn't have had such
valuables on board when she sank, would she?'

'The pirates may not have taken everything,' she
argued.

'Perhaps not.' He was silent for a few moments then said, 'The privateer's ship was called the *Pelican*, wasn't it?'

'So our records show. Her owner and master was commissioned by King William III of England together with some other aristocrats with interests in these islands to intercept and seize pirate ships operating in the islands. He must have turned pirate himself, seized the *Santiago* and made off with the loot.'

'He didn't get very far with it,' drawled Kit drily. 'His ship and all the loot were caught in a hurricane and sank.'

'How do you know? We can find no record of what happened to him in our archives. Where did you hear that story? Is it based on fact?'

'I believe so,' he drawled.

'I suppose you're interested in him because his name was Barlow. You don't really believe he was an ancestor of yours, do you?' she said derisively.

His teeth flashed in his shadowed face as he grinned down at her.

'Sure, I do. Nathaniel Barlow turned up in Charleston, South Carolina soon after the sinking of the *Santiago* and established a trading business there. He had a small fleet of ships and traded with the islands and his grandson founded the Barlow shipping line. My brother and I aren't direct descendants of his because the main branch of the family died out but our great-grandfather was descended from one of old Nathaniel's sons and he inherited the business when his cousin died. My father was really keen on genealogy and that sort of thing, kept all the letters and records pertaining to the beginnings of the company and even drew up a family tree.'

'Where is all this information?'

'Locked up in a file in the Charleston office.'

'Brian and I would love to see it. Do you think we could?'

'You'd have to apply in writing to my brother,' he replied coolly. He raised his head sharply and turned towards the shadowy palms that leaned over the pathway she would take up to the resort buildings.

'What's the matter?' she asked.

'I thought I heard someone breathing in the shadows.' He turned back to her. 'You'd better go back to your room. If you don't want Professor Haines to know we've met before, the less we're seen alone together the better, and now we've had this talk we can go on pretending we've never met until this morning. It shouldn't be too difficult. Do you agree?'

'I agree we should continue to pretend we've never met before,' she said stiffly, keeping to herself the observation that she was going to find it difficult even if he didn't. 'I suppose you've left your yacht in St Thomas?'

'Yes, at the marina there.'

'And your wife? Did you leave her on board the yacht?' She tried to ask the question casually but even to her own ears her voice sounded rather sharp.

He turned to face her fully and moonlit shone on his features, lighting them up for the first time, showing her that he was both surprised and puzzled by by question.

'What's this?' he queried, the left corner of his lips quirking in amusement. 'What wife? I don't have a wife. I'm not married and never have been. Strictly single, that's me. Have you forgotten?'

She remembered a leggy young woman with blonde hair and a clear voice ringing out: Now we can be married. Now we can set the date.

'But I thought——' she began and broke off. He didn't know she had seen him being greeted by Sherri.

'What did you think?' he asked softly, tilting his head forward, peering at her face as if trying to see the expression on it. He was too near now for her peace of mind. She could smell the scents of his tanned skin, hear the steady muted throb of his heart. She longed suddenly to touch him, to slide her hands inside his shirt-opening, to feel the smoothness of his skin. She stepped back quickly before temptation overwhelmed her.

'Oh, I just thought that you might have a wife now you're a respectable businessman,' she said lightly. 'A wife and children.'

'I'm no more respectable now than I have ever been,' he retorted with a laugh at his own expense. 'And I don't have a wife. But I guess what you're really trying to find out is if there have been any women in my life since you left. Well, there have been a couple but . . .'

'No. That isn't what I wanted to know,' she interrupted him. 'I'm not interested in our love life. I just want to make sure you won't tell Brian or Harriet that you and I used to know each other.'

'And I've already said that I won't,' he retorted, as sharp as she had been. 'But I can't promise your professor will never know about our flash-in-the-pan affair. All I can promise is that he'll never hear about it from me. Good night.'

He left her abruptly, to walk swiftly in the direction of the jetty and Stella turned on to the pathway that led up to the building where her bedroom was located. She hadn't gone very far when a figure stepped out from the trees.

'Who's there?' Harriet's voice challenged.

'Me. Stella.'

'But you went to bed. What are you doing wandering about at this time of the night?' Harriet came up to her, peered up at her face.

'What time is it?' asked Stella, repressing a sharp retort. What was Harriet doing wandering about?

'After midnight,' Harriet replied.

'I went for a walk. I couldn't rest and I thought the air would clear my headache. I walked along to the end of the beach.' Stella began to walk on along the path to the courtyard in front of the building. A light over each doorway illuminated the flagstones of the yard and the leaves and blossoms of the shrubs.

'So it was you we could see. I said as much to Brian,' breathed Harriet, hurrying to keep up with her.

'You and Brian saw me?' repeated Stella. As they reached the courtyard she stopped and turned to look at the other woman.

'Sure we did. He and I walked down to the jetty with Gerry and Matt when they left. Brian wanted a word with Kit. But he wasn't on board the ship. And then as we came off the jetty on our way back we thought we saw two people loitering on the beach. Who was with you? Kit?'

'If you'd waited for us to reach the jetty you'd have seen it was him,' replied Stella coldly, finding her room key and stepping up on to the veranda to fit it into the lock of her door. 'And then Brian could have had his word with Kit,' she added drily.

She wondered if it had been Harriet Kit had heard breathing in the shadows and perhaps Brian had been there too. The suspicion that all she and Kit had said to each other before he had left her had been overheard chilled her to the marrow.

'Yes, I guess he could have,' admitted Harriet. 'But we weren't really sure it was him. Or you, for that matter. And Brian was tired. He wanted to get to bed to be fit for diving in the morning.' She paused tilting her head to one side and glanced at Stella out of the corners of her eyes. 'Is it true? Are you and Brian going to be married when you go back to England?'

'It's true. Did he tell you we are tonight?'

'Uhuh. Must say I was surprised. Seems to me it would be a most unsuitable marriage.'

'Why?' Stella turned back from the opened door. 'How can you say that? What do you know about us? You don't know either of us very well. You and I have just met and——'

'I don't know you, I agree,' Harriet retorted. 'But I know Brian. He used to visit Larry often, was out here two years ago diving and exploring wrecks with Larry. I know him well enough to know that in choosing you to be his wife he's made a mistake. Another mistake like the first choice of wife he made.' Harriet's voice rasped jeeringly and turning away she walked off and was swallowed up by the dark shadows of the trees.

In her room Stella clicked on the bedside lamp, put the chain on the door and began to undress. The unexpected meeting with Harriet had ruffled her. She was convinced now Harriet had been hiding in the trees close to herself and Kit just before he had left her. She shivered with revulsion. She hated the thought of being spied on. If Harriet had heard everything she and Kit had said, the woman knew now that they had met before and had had an affair. A flash-in-the-pan affair, Kit had called it. He had let her know in no uncertain terms what he thought of her nine months' stay with him. It had been so short, so unimportant in his life, it wasn't worth mentioning.

But now Harriet knew about it. What she had hoped to prevent happening had happened. Harriet knew and, if Brian had been with her in the shadows, he knew. Unless he had left Harriet to go to bed before she and Kit had reached the end of the jetty.

But even if Brian had gone to bed and hadn't overheard the conversation between herself and Kit, if he hadn't been with Harriet he would soon know. Harriet would see to that. She would tell him everything she had overheard.

Oh, why had she bothered to go and ask Kit to be quiet about their affair? Stella wondered miserably, as she slid into bed and settled her head on the pillow. She should have left well alone. She should have trusted in Kit's natural reticence about himself instead of seeking him out to ask him to deny he had ever met her before. She should have guessed that their affair had been so unimportant to him—one of several probably in his life—that he would never refer to it or tell a stranger about it.

He wasn't married. He hadn't married Sherri. Why? Had Sherri found out that he had spent nine months living in close quarters on his yacht with another woman, taken umbrage and jilted him? During the time she had wandered about the islands with him she had discovered he had many acquaintances on the islands: divers, yachtsmen, marina owners, dockmasters, socialites many of whom had seen her in his company and on his yacht. One of them could easily have told someone else who had told Sherri about the English woman living with Kit Barlow, who was his mate, his mistress . . .

If only she had known he hadn't married Sherri, if only she had known. No, it was no use going off on that tack. No good could come of such conjecture. She had believed at the time he had planned to marry Sherri when he returned to Nassau and she had acted accordingly. She had packed her bags and left him and he had made no attempt to persuade her to stay because they had arranged to split at the end of nine months. He hadn't wanted her to stay on. He hadn't been in love with her. A flash-in-the-pan, their affair had been for him and nine months of her company had been enough. If only it had been like that for her.

But she had believed she was well on the way to being cured of him until she had been kissed by him tonight. Now she was wondering how she was going to get through the next few days until Jack Cowan came, seeing Kit every day, hearing his voice. How was she going to hide from him and from Brian and Harriet the fact that she was still in love with him? What was she going to say to Brian when he asked her if it was true what Harriet had told him she had overheard tonight? What was she going to do . . .?

She fell asleep before she had decided what to do but woke next morning knowing exactly what she would do if Brian brought up the matter of her affair with Kit. She would tell him the truth and if he didn't like it he could withdraw his proposal to marry her.

She was early in the dining-room but not before Brian, Kit, Gerry and Matt who were all breakfasting together and being waited on by the fussy Harriet, who had a way of touching each man on the shoulder and leaning over him in a confidential way, pressuring him to have more to eat, more coffee, as if his welfare was all important to her. Particularly did she linger over Kit almost possessively.

'No headache, this morning, I hope,' Brian greeted her, pulling out a chair for her.

'None. I feel great,' she said. 'And you?'

'Raring to go diving,' he replied.

He smiled at her and she felt relief rush through her. She was sure now he knew nothing about her and Kit. Perhaps Harriet hadn't had time to speak to him alone this morning.

'I took a walk along the beach before turning in last night and that took care of the headache,' she said lightly, shaking out her table napkin, giving him an opening to say he had seen her walking with Kit. 'After that I slept like a log.'

'Good.' He smiled at her again and went on to talk about his plans for the morning's dive, mentioning the freighter. 'We don't have to bother with exploring inside that. It was cleared out long ago. Apparently it was British and was holed on the reef before World War Two. Of course, being made of steel it has only rusted and been covered with barnacles. I suspect the hull of the *Santiago* was pretty well broken up and scattered by the surge.'

'More of it may have been buried in the sand,' said Stella.

'Well, we'll soon found out,' said Brian.

'See you both at the ship in about half an hour?' suggested Kit. He had stood up and was pushing his chair under the table. Gerry and Matt had already left. Kit didn't look at Stella nor had he greeted her when she sat down.

'We'll be there,' replied Brian.

Kit left the dining-room and Harriet came bustling in with Stella's breakfast.

'The girl who usually waits at table in the morning is sick today so I'm waitress,' she said brightly.

'Are you coming with us this morning?' asked Brian.

'Not today, Brian dear. Today I must do my accounts. And then I'm expecting another group of fishermen to fly in this afternoon. I'll come another day. How do you feel this morning, Stella? Headache gone?'

She leaned over Stella, put a hand on her shoulder. Stella looked up at the square tanned face. She looked into the small grey eyes and saw nothing in them, no expression of concern. They seemed as cold and hard as lead pellets.

'Yes, thanks,' Stella replied. 'The walk I took along the beach last night cleared my head. She glanced at Brian. 'I met Harriet when I was coming back from my walk last night. She told me you and she were out for a walk too and saw me on the beach with Kit Barlow.'

It was another opening for him to say something about having seen her and having overheard part of her conversation with Kit. He looked across at her, his eyebrows crimped in an expression of puzzlement but before he could say anything Harriet rushed into speech.

'Oh, I didn't say we were sure it was you or Kit. We were too far away for us to be sure, weren't we, Brian?'

'I . . . I can't seem to recall,' he was beginning slowly when Harriet cut in again forcibly.

'We just assumed it was you and Kit. You must excuse me now. I have to talk to Virginia, give her instructions about tonight's dinner.'

Smiling her bright yet insincere smile Harriet hurried away. The door to the kitchen swung to and fro for a few seconds after the speed of her exit.

'She is the most amazing person,' Brian said smiling, his glance returning to Stella after he had watched Harriet leave the room. He didn't seem to have noticed that Harriet had spoken for him. 'A bundle of energy. She runs this place single handed, deals with all types of people, some of them really tough characters. And the island people who work for her adore her.'

'She was telling me that if she doesn't get someone to go in with her she might go bankrupt,' said Stella.

'I fear so,' Brian sighed and shook his head from side to side sadly. 'It's costing more and more to keep a place like this in good repair, far away from everywhere as it is, everything having to be brought in from other islands or from the States. She was showing me the maintenance bills yesterday. They're horrific. I think she's hoping that we can find something that will prove conclusively that a Spanish galleon was wrecked near here and then more tourists who like diving around wrecks will want to stay at this resort.'

'You mean she'll use our exploration as a way of publicising the resort?'

'Right. So I hope we find some really good artefacts. Some which could only have been on the *Santiago*.'

'Such as a piece of wood with its name carved into it,' suggested Stella drily. 'Or an old cannon or two which could only have been forged in Spain at the beginning of the eighteenth century. Finding shards of pottery or some glassware isn't going to prove that the *Santiago*'s remains are under that freighter. The treasure, the identifiable jewellery belonging to passengers, was probably all looted.'

'I know that. Except the pieces Larry found.' He looked very worried for a moment then with an effort shook off his anxiety. 'But the sooner we get started the sooner we'll find something. Are you ready to go to the ship, yet?'

'Yes, I'm ready,' she said, laying down her knife and fork and wiping her lips. Since he hadn't referred to the walk she had taken last night with Kit she could only guess he wasn't at all interested or concerned about her nocturnal rendezvous with another man so she decided not to raise the matter again. Let sleeping dogs lie, she thought with a wry grin. No point in stirring up trouble where there wasn't any.

CHAPTER FOUR

LEAVING the gully between the coral outgrowths where she had been searching all morning, hanging weightless above golden sand and probing delicately in it, hoping to come across some small or large artefact or more time-encrusted timbers, Stella slowly began her ascent. Above her the surface of the sea heaved and rippled like molten silver and shoals of fish shimmered past her as she drifted upwards with the help of her buoyancy compensator which she had filled with air to counteract the lead weights at her waist, passing between overhanging cliffs of coral where gorgonians, graceful fans of hardened polyps, flourished like tiny petrified trees.

It was the third day of diving and although she had found no artefacts at the supposed site of the wreck of the *Santiago* she had taken pleasure as always in the life beneath the surface of the sea. It was so wonderful to dive again in warm, clear water and to renew her acquaintance with the fish and underwater growths with which she had become familiar during her cruise among the Caribbean islands with Kit. As then, she was now amazed by the brilliant colours of the marine fantasy world, the orange cup corals, the yellow tube sponges, the glowing purples, blues and scarlets of fish.

She broke surface close to the *Sea Urchin* and after taking off her flippers and handing them to Gerry who had surfaced before her, she climbed

up the ladder on to the afterdeck and he helped
her to remove the scuba tank from her back.
Beyond him she could see Brian in serious
conversation with Kit. Beneath her feet, the deck
lurched as the ship rolled on a heavy surge that
was washing into the cove and she realised that
while they had been diving a strong wind had
gusted up, blowing right into the cove and making
the anchorage uncomfortable.

'Well? Any luck?' Brian, still in his tropical
diving suit, a rubberised, long-sleeved one-piece that
left the legs bare, turned towards her. His tousled
hair was still soaking wet, dripping water down his
cheeks and he was frowning. She recognised the
expression of disappointment on his face.

'Nothing,' she said, shaking her head and
unbuckling the weight belt from her hips, her
glance going stealthily to Kit. Straight and tall, his
curling hair glowing in the bright sunlight he was
immaculate in white shirt and khaki shorts and, as
always when she saw him, she felt the flame of
naked desire uncurl within her. She looked quickly
away from him at Brian and the flame flickered
uneasily and died down. There was nothing in
Brian's appearance to arouse her desire. 'Nothing,'
she repeated.

The expression of disappointment and frustra-
tion on Brian's face increased. He looked suddenly
old and careworn, and sympathy blossomed in
Stella.

'But maybe we'll have some luck this afternoon,'
she said, linking an arm through his.

'We won't be diving this afternoon,' he said
tersely. 'Can't you see the surge that's running? It
isn't safe for the dive-ship to be anchored here.
Barlow is getting out of here as soon as he can

weigh anchor.'

She realised then that Kit had gone up to the
wheelhouse and that Gerry and Matt had both
gone forward to winch in the anchor. The engines
throbbed, the anchor came up and *Sea Urchin*
lunged forward into the crested, green waves, away
from the sun-sparkled cove and its dangerous,
ship-wrecking reefs.

Harriet, too, had difficulty in hiding her
disappointment when they told her, as they all ate
lunch in the resort dining-room, that once again
they had come up with nothing from the sea-bed
and Stella guessed the woman was worried about
the cost of the venture. The longer the dive-ship
was there the more she would have to pay out to
Jack Cowan's salvaging company.

'What are you going to do?' Harriet asked,
sinking down into a spare chair at the table, her
grey eyes gazing at Brian.

'Immediately, I'm going to study Larry's notes
again,' he replied, 'to make sure I haven't missed
anything. And then I'm going to go through the
copies I made of the account of the seizing and
scuttling of the *Santiago* that was made by one of
the crew of the galleon when he managed to get
back to Spain. I found it in the archives of Spanish
maritime history in Madrid. The account is clear
and concise and it was in it that I found reference
to Nathaniel Barlow being the pirate. With the
account, there was a list of the passengers, the
cargo she was carrying, her port of embarkation
and her destination. She left Cadiz in July 1702
bound for Havana.'

'Does the account say she was seized near
Sanada?' asked Kit. Usually at any conference
they had about the expedition he maintained an

attitude of indifference, as if he wasn't interested or as if he didn't want to get involved in an argument with Brian.

'The island isn't named. Probably it didn't have a name then,' said Brian. 'But the description given fits it. Low-lying, made of coral, surrounded by dangerous shallows and reefs and set miles apart from the other islands in the chain, as if it didn't belong to them. And you have to agree Sanada is different from the other islands in the area. It's the only one in this part of the Caribbean that isn't volcanic. Sometimes I like to fancy it's a Bahamian island that has dragged its anchor and drifted this way.'

'Did Larry Lundgren ever test that area with a magnetometer? asked Kit.

'What is that?' put in Harriet quickly.

'It's an electrical device. You explore the surface of the water with it and it picks up messages from any unusual mass of iron on the bottom. There would be iron fastenings on the galleon and also the cannon would have been forged from iron. I assume the information you have about the ship includes the number of cannon she was armed with?' said Kit turning to Brian again.

'Yes, it does. I don't remember the exact number, offhand, but she had cannon. The answer to your other question is no. Larry didn't use a magnetometer. He was convinced, you see, that the wreck lay under the wreck of the freighter so using the magnetometer on the surface would only have picked up the iron from which that was built,' said Brian. He sighed. 'Well, I think I'll go to my room and read those accounts again,' he added rising to his feet. 'And we'll try again tomorrow morning.' He glanced at Kit who had sat back in his chair, the expression of bland indifference on his face again. 'If,' Brian went on rather diffidently, 'if you have any suggestions about where we should explore, I'd like to hear them, Barlow.'

'I'll let you know if I think of anything,' drawled Kit.

'Perhaps we should use the airlift,' said Stella. 'Suck out some of the sand and debris that is in the gully. It might reveal something.'

'Good idea,' said Brian, patting her shoulder. 'We'll try that tomorrow morning. All right with you, Barlow?'

'Sure,' said Kit laconically, getting up. Gerry and Matt had already left the table and were playing darts in the bar. He turned away and strolled over to them.

'What will you do this afternoon, Stella?' Brian asked.

'I'd really like to phone my sister, Audrey. I said I'd let her know I'd got here safely.' She looked at Harriet, who was beginning to collect up dishes from the table. 'Is there a phone on the island?' she asked.

'Yes, at the telephone station in the village,' replied Harriet. 'Thirty-five miles away. Kit is driving in this afternoon. He also wants to make a call to Jack Cowan in St Thomas. I've lent him the truck. You could go with him.'

'Will I be able to make a long-distance call to England?' asked Stella, wondering whether it would be wise to go with Kit.

'Sure you will. Just give Leonie—she's the telephone operator—the number you want and she'll get through to the exchange at Roadtown, the capital of the islands, and they'll try the English number ...' Harriet turned and bustled across the lounge. 'Kit,' she called, 'Kit. Stella wants to make a phone call too. She can go in with you, can't she, to the village? You won't mind having her company?'

Kit turned slowly and looked across at Stella, his lean, tanned face impassive although the blue eyes seemed to leap and dance with blazing light. Once before, long ago, he had looked at her across a room and her heart had jumped in her breast as it did now.

'Now, I won't mind,' he said coolly, ignoring Harriet and speaking directly to Stella. 'How soon will you be ready to go?'

It wouldn't be safe to go with him, Stella warned herself. It would be best to stay at the resort, spend the afternoon with Brian going through the accounts of the galleon's ship-wreck. But she took no notice of the warning, acknowledging to herself that she had been longing to be alone with Kit again ever since he had kissed her the other night on the beach. She didn't want to stay with Brian or to read the copies of historical documents. She wanted to be with Kit, longed and ached in every fibre of her body to be with him, to talk freely to him, away from Harriet's watchful, suspicious eyes.

'Five minutes?' she asked lightly.

'See you outside, then,' Kit replied coolly, and turned away to say something to Gerry.

Stella turned also, to speak to Brian, but he was walking away from the dining-room towards the doorway that led to Harriet's office and Harriet was beside him, short and plump, her gilt-blonde head no higher than Brian's shoulder, and he wasn't a tall man, her right hand at his left elbow as if guiding him while she whispered to him confidentially. Harriet was probably talking to him about the wreck, perhaps expressing her disappointment because no more artefacts had been discovered, thought Stella as she slid back one of the screens that covered the glass doors that overlooked the terrace and stepped outside. Yes, Harriet must be very worried about the failure of the diving expedition so far.

In her bedroom she changed from the white trousers and T-shirt she had been wearing and into a wrapover skirt of bright, printed cotton and a plain white sleeveless blouse. Her hair was dry now, after the morning's diving operation and swung silkily about her shoulders as she left the room quickly and almost ran along the pathway under the palms. She felt light-hearted in a way she hadn't experienced for a long time, like a person feels when let out of school or work. For a short time she was going to 'goof off' with Kit, share an hour or so of stolen delight with him . . .

Oh, no. Her footsteps slowed decorously. She stopped swinging her shoulder-bag. She mustn't let it show, this joy that would keep bubbling up in her. She mustn't let him see how she felt about driving into the village with him. She must remember he wouldn't feel the same way.

He was already sitting in the driver's seat of the dark blue truck which was parked on the wide driveway in front of the main resort building. The engine was running and as soon as she slammed the door shut after climbing up into the seat beside him, he pushed the gear lever into first, then second and the truck trundled down to the entrance of the driveway and on to the rough road, passing the small airstrip.

Rock music blared out of the radio in the

dashboard. The noise irritated Stella and she wished he would switch it off. She would have asked him to do so but she wasn't going to speak first. So she sat in silence, looking out at the palms and bushes edging the bright, sunlit ribbon of the road as it curved round following the shoreline of the wide bay. It was hot in front of the truck and she could feel sweat beginning to start on her skin. There didn't seem to be any air-conditioning. She noticed the window beside Kit was wound right down so she wound down the window beside her and hoped the draught wafting in would cool her.

Bright and glittery was the water of the bay, a brilliant turquoise dotted with silvery-white waves, churned up by the stiff breeze, broke. Then the road made a sudden turn to the right away from the shoreline and they bumped over its uneven surface past the gardens and gateways of houses hidden from sight among clusters of casuarinas and palms.

'The private hideaways of the wealthy,' remarked Kit drily. 'Sanada also has its share of escapees from the frozen north who have bought land cheaply here and had villas built where they can spend six months of the year.'

'Have you ever been to this island before?' she asked.

'Once. On a diving trip,' he replied shortly. He slanted a sidelong glance at her. 'The professor seems to be disappointed with the lack of result from your searches under the freighter.'

'So am I,' she sighed.

'Has it occurred to either of you that you might be looking in the wrong place?'

'We've been looking where Professor Lundgren indicated we should look.'

'I know that. But there are the remains of a wooden ship on the other side of the reef,' he drawled casually.

'How do you know?'

'What do you think I've been doing while you've been diving? Twiddling my thumbs in the wheelhouse?' His voice rasped scornfully. 'I've been diving too. The first day I went down just for fun to explore the reef, look at the coral, play with the fish. There's a big outgrowth of coral on the other side, fairly recent I would think. I dived under it and found part of a wooden hull lying on the sand. The second time I went down I poked about. This came rolling out of the wreck.' He tossed something into her lap.

It was heavy. She looked down. It was a round lead ball. She touched it with one finger.

'Looks like a musket ball,' she said.

'Right first time. It was encrusted with coral and other growths. I cleaned it up. There are cannonballs down there by the wreck too.'

'But why haven't you told Brian? Why haven't you shown this to him?'

'Why should I? He and you have permission to search under the freighter not the other side of the reef.'

The truck trundled on, swerving violently when a pot-hole yawned suddenly in the rough surface of the road. They passed a few native houses, some obviously new and built in a contemporary bungalow style, some little more than wooden shacks, their timbers grey with age, their window-frames sagging. In a garden beside one of the bungalows two people were weeding between rows of vegetables, a man and a woman. Hearing the truck, they straightened up and waved, their black-

skinned arms shining in the sunlight, their white
teeth flashing in dark faces. Kit and Stella waved
back.

'You've told me. What makes you think I won't
tell him?' asked Stella.

'You can do what you like with the information,'
he replied coolly. 'But I'm not saying anything to
him until I've been in touch with Jack.' He paused
for a moment then went on, 'I've got this gut
feeling there's something very fishy about the
Lundgren–Haines underwater exploration.' His
grin flashed briefly. 'And I didn't mean to make a
pun.'

'So what do you mean?' she asked, turning the
musket ball between her hands.

'I mean that I think neither Professor Haines
nor Harriet Lundgren are being entirely straightforward. I think they haven't levelled with you or
me about what they hope to find in the crevasse
under that freighter. They probably haven't
levelled with the local government or the archaeological museum in England either.'

'I'm afraid I don't understand what you're
getting at,' she said defensively.

'OK. I'll put it more bluntly. I'm guessing that
they hope to find treasure and when it is found, by
Haines, of course, they won't tell us or the
government but will share it between themselves.'

'But you said yourself the other night that we
wouldn't find much in the way of valuables
because the *Santiago* had been looted before she
sank,' she argued.

'Maybe it wasn't the *Santiago* that was wrecked
on this particular reef. Maybe it was the *Pelican*.
That would account for the name of the peninsula
of land and the resort, wouldn't it? The island

could have been where old Nat Barlow used to hang out, lurking in the cove behind the reef to pounce on passing ships. The island is situated on one of the main routes from the Atlantic and Europe.' He paused again as if waiting for her to make a comment but when she didn't continued, 'If it was the *Pelican* that was wrecked, there would be treasure to be found, wouldn't there?'

'But Professor Lundgren was quite sure it was the *Santiago*,' she argued. 'In his notes he stated quite definitely he'd found timbers belonging to it.'

'How do we know he wasn't lying when he made those notes?' replied Kit. 'How do we know he didn't lie about the position of the wreck? He could have made the suggestion that he had found the remains of a looted galleon so as to hide the fact that he had discovered the wreck of the privateer, the master and crew of which had done the looting, hidden in an entirely different place.'

Stella was silent, horrified by what he was suggesting. She rolled the musket ball in her hands. The road swung to the left and the bay came into view, water shimmering in the bright sunlight.

'I suppose you're going to tell Jack Cowan that you suspect Harriet and Brian are in a conspiracy together to find treasure and keep it to themselves without declaring it,' she said at last.

'I am.'

They had reached the outskirts of the village. Small houses appeared on one side of the road. On the other side a beach overhung with palms curved beside the greenish-blue water of the bay. A wharf of dark piles jutted out from the land and beside it a blue freighter was docked.

'Harriet said the telephone station was at the top of the street going up from the wharf, so I guess this is it,' murmured Kit and swung the truck into a narrow street lined with small houses, each one in a garden bursting with plants and blazing with colour. At the top of the street a white painted church with a steeple gleamed against the blue sky. Next to the church was a yellow shed with a red roof to which a steel tower was attached: the microwave tower by which all telephone communication was made.

'You go in and make your call first,' said Kit. 'I want to go down to the wharf. That freighter looks like a Barlow ship. I might as well check it out.'

Stella jumped down from the truck, slammed the door shut and walked through the wide-open door of the yellow shed. Inside there was only one room. It was occupied by a broad-shouldered black woman. She was dressed in a sleeveless cream-coloured dress and her hair was twisted into tiny tight plaits all over her head. She was seated at a table on which there was a telephone. She nodded at Stella and said in beautifully pronounced English, 'Can I help you?'

'I'd like to make a phone call to England, please. Is that possible?'

'It is possible. Please give me the number you want to call, the name of the person you wish to speak to. Do you wish to pay for the call now or do you wish to use your international telephone credit card number?'

Stella said she would pay after she had made the call, gave the number and her sister's name. The woman wrote everything down on a pad before her. Then, after indicating that Stella should sit

down on one of the chairs provided she picked up
the receiver of the phone on the table and dialled.
In a few seconds she was speaking, giving all the
information to someone on the other end of the
line. That done she set down the receiver and said
to Stella, 'When the Roadtown operator reaches
the number you want, the phone in that kiosk over
there will ring. Go into the kiosk, pick up the
phone and speak into it. The party you are calling
will answer.' The woman smiled for the first time.
'Are you on holiday here?'

'Yes, I am.'

'Where are you staying?'

'At the Pelican's Roost.'

'Ah yes, with Harriet. I hope you are
comfortable. My cousin, Virginia, is the cook
there. You find the meals good?'

'Very good.'

Footsteps sounded on the path outside. A man's
figure darkened the doorway. He spoke to the
telephone operator in the local lilting accent which
Stella had difficulty in understanding even though
the language spoken was English.

'You will have to wait, Sam,' said the telephone
operator. 'This lady is before you.' She smiled at
Stella. 'Sam is my brother. He has the toothache
badly and wants to make an appointment with the
dentist in Roadtown.'

The man sat down on a chair and for a while the
conversation was all about toothache and what to
do for it when you couldn't get to a dentist easily.
Stella learned that Sam was manager and owner of
the village hotel, that the freighter down at the
dock was a Barlow ship and had brought the
monthly cargo of frozen meat and other foods,
hardware, furniture and liquor from Florida.

'Don't you get any goods from Britain?'

'Oh, yes. If you go into the grocery store you will see English marmalade on the shelves, English canned goods,' said Leonie, and just then the telephone in the kiosk rang. 'Go now. Go in and pick it up,' she said and lifted her receiver.

Stella was soon talking to her sister. The call lasted only a few minutes. Stella paid for it and after thanking the operator she stepped outside into the hot sunshine, to await Kit's return.

As soon as the truck stopped in front of the building she walked out from under the trees where she had been sheltering from the sun's rays and went up to Kit as he came towards the telephone station.

'I've been thinking about what you said to me about Brian and Harriet being in some sort of conspiracy together to find treasure and not declare it,' she whispered. She put out a hand and laid it on his arm. Her fingers curled in instant pleasure at the feel of silken hairs and the tensing of hard muscle. 'I'm sure Brian wouldn't be a party to anything underhand. I'm sure he wouldn't.'

He glanced down at her, his eyes narrow chips of blue ice. Then he looked at her hand. He took hold of it lifted it from his arm and dropped it as if it were something distasteful to him. 'How do I know you're not in the conspiracy too,' he gibed nastily.

'You'll just have to take my word that I'm not,' she retorted, lifting her head proudly. 'But please wait before telling Jack Cowan of your suspicions. Please, Kit. I could swear Brian is honest, possibly too honest for his own good.'

'You're bound to defend him,' he replied. 'You're going to marry him.'

'But that isn't why I'm defending him. He's honest, I'm sure he is. And he wouldn't damage his reputation as a professional archaeologist by becoming involved in any conspiracy.'

'Wouldn't he?' His eyebrows went up in satirical surprise. 'You'd be surprised what the thought of finding treasure will do to a man. Gold for free has a way of warping the most honest person. OK, I won't say anything to Jack yet. But I have to phone him to find out if he's recovered from his flu, and if he can come out here and take over from me. The sooner the better for you and me, don't you think? Once Jack's here I'll be able to leave and then you won't have to pretend you and I have never met before.'

He walked past her into the telephone station. Feeling suddenly listless Stella climbed up into the front of the truck to sit and wait for him. Her holiday feeling, that up-soaring of spirits she had felt at the thought of spending a couple of hours with him had soon evaporated and now she felt depressed because he obviously didn't want to be alone with her. He was itching to leave Sanada, hoping that Jack Cowan would be well enough to take over soon, in a day or two perhaps, and then it would be over, the excitement and strain of seeing him every day, of hearing his voice and of longing in the night to be alone with him again in the hopes of recapturing the delight they had once shared together.

So far Brian had said nothing to her about the possibility of her having met and known Kit before she had come to Sanada and as a result she could only assume, with relief, that Harriet hadn't overheard any part of the conversation between herself and Kit before they had parted that first night. And Kit had been very careful, keeping aloof from her, never speaking to her. But, then, perhaps he didn't want to be near her or speak to her. Perhaps he hadn't found it hard to pretend because he had another lover now, waiting for him in St Thomas. Even though he had said there was no one on board his yacht he hadn't denied he had had company on his shake-down cruise. Yes, that must be the reason why he could be so aloof. He had another woman so he didn't want her. And she had Brian, didn't she? So why should she want Kit?

The other door of the truck opened abruptly, Kit climbed in, slammed the door shut and started the engine. The truck rolled away from the telephone station down the narrow village road.

'Did you get through to Jack Cowan?' Stella asked.

'Yes, he's up and about and should be able to fly out here tomorrow, maybe.' He glanced at her. 'You look hot. Like to go swimming?'

'Where?'

'There are other beaches besides the one at the resort. I remember one from the last time I was here. It's beyond the village at the north-western tip of the island. It's quite secluded.' He braked the truck at the junction of the lane with the main coast road.

'I haven't got my swimsuit with me.'

'That never used to stop you from swimming as I recall,' he said drily. 'I don't have mine either. Well, what do you say? Would you like to go? Or are you just dying to return to your dear professor? God, he's as dry as the dust on some ancient artefact found in a desert.' His voice rasped harshly. 'And I can't understand why you're going to marry him.'

'I like and respect him. He has a very fine intellect and we have much in common,' she retorted. Then with an attempt at lightness, she added, 'Besides he's the only man who has ever asked me to marry him. He likes and respects me.'

His eyes glinted with a strange expression before they looked away from her face to glance out of the windscreen.

'So what is it to be? A swim at the cove I mentioned? Or back to the resort?' he asked.

This would be the only time she would have alone with him before he left, her one chance to steal some delight with him.

'I'd like to go to the cove,' she said and at once his foot came off the brake and the truck surged forward to turn to the right instead of to the left.

Once the village was left behind, the road meandered through the bush. There was no sign of habitation and after a few miles the road ended abruptly, becoming only a narrow track along which no car or truck could be driven.

Kit parked the truck and they got out to force their way through the bushes. Spiky twigs snatched at their clothing and bare arms and legs. At last they reached a beach of thick coarse sand, a narrow semi-circle of sunlit gold rimming the clear, greenish water of what was really a small lagoon, protected from surf by a coral reef so that only the tiniest of ripples showed on its surface. Some small palms and sea-grape trees leaned over the sand.

Stella would have made some comment to Kit about the perfection of the place but he strode away from her into the shelter of some trees and reappeared in a few seconds without his clothing to run straight down to the water. Lifting his arms above his head he plunged under the surface, reappearing several yards out to swim strongly towards the distant reef.

She discarded her own clothing with less abandon, leaving it in a neat pile before also running into the water and diving. The water was warm but tingling with salt, refreshing on her hot skin, washing away the pinpricks of heat rash; washing away too the feeling of depression.

By the time she reached the reef Kit had left it to swim back to the shore and she wondered if he was trying to avoid being close to her. After resting a few moments, treading water, she swam back slowly to the beach, shaking back her hair as she walked out of the water, squeezing it as dry as she could.

'That was lovely,' she murmured as she sat down on the sand beside Kit who, as naked as he had been when swimming, was lying prone on his opened out shirt, his head resting on his folded arms. Droplets of water, reflecting the sunlight, spangled his hair. He didn't answer her.

In the golden light of the westering sun his skin looked bronze. She admired the symmetrical shape of his torso, the broad swimmer's shoulders tapering to the waist and wondered what he would do if she touched him, stroked her hand over the pads of muscle under the gleaming skin and down his spine. The thought of caressing him rekindled the flame of desire within her. It flared up painfully, seeming to scorch through her.

'Kit,' she wanted to say, 'oh, Kit, do you remember when we used to swim and make love afterwards? I wish we could do that again. I wish we could have that time again.'

But she said nothing of what she thought. She

had less control, however, over her actions than
she had over her speech. Her hand went out and
touched his shoulder, fingers spreading out over it.
He turned his head, looked round at her, his slitted
blue glance raking her bare body, also gilded by
sunlight to pale gold. With a growled oath he
reached up an arm and pulled her down beside
him.

The coarse sand grazed her fine skin but she
didn't care because his mouth, hot and hungry,
was covering hers. It had come. That moment of
delight she had longed for. Parting her lips to the
pressure of his, she slid her hands into his hair and,
moving her body against his temptingly, let go the
last remnant of control, her mind reeling under the
onslaught of her own desire.

Then, quite rudely, she was shocked out of the
tender, sensual mood. His hands instead of
holding her and caressing her were pushing her
away from him and his lips had gone from hers
wrenched away brutally. He sprang to his feet and
left her lying on the sand, abandoned like a piece
of debris washed up by the tide and left high and
dry, her desires unfulfilled.

Feeling shattered by his sudden desertion of her,
she sat up, clasping her arms about her breasts,
wondering if perhaps he had heard someone
coming. But there was no one else on the beach.
The cove was still empty, sunlit and silent, the
sand gleaming gold, the water glinting turquoise.

Fully dressed in shirt and shorts Kit stepped out
of the trees. He didn't come towards her, only
called to her.

'Hurry up and get dressed,' he ordered roughly.
'It's past four o'clock. Time we went back. Harriet
will start getting suspicious.'

Swinging away from her he walked into the bush. Bewildered by his coldness she dressed quickly and followed him. Soon they were seated side by side in the truck as it sped over the rough road.

She wanted to ask him what had gone wrong, why he had withdrawn from her so cruelly at the moment when passion had been red hot between them and culmination so close. But pride forbade that she should ask so she waited for him to speak and make some sort of explanation.

He didn't speak and they drove on in silence through the village and out on to the road to the resort. It was a silence that vibrated with tension, with all their unspoken thoughts and all their churned-up emotions. Yet not until the truck had been parked in the driveway of the resort and they were both walking away from it was Stella able to force herself to question him, breaking through the barrier of her pride.

'Why, Kit, why did you withdraw like that?' she whispered.

He turned to face her. His face, gilded by sunlight, looked like a mask beaten from bronze.

'You really want to know?' he queried.

'Yes, I do. You were so violent.' Her voice shook a little. 'It hurt.'

'It was meant to,' he said nastily. 'I don't like being used.'

'I don't understand.'

'Don't you?' His eyes were as empty and cold as Arctic seas. 'You were using me. You're sex-starved, Stella, darling. And what you can't get from your dried-up professor you were hoping you could get from me, for old times' sake.'

'I'm not ... I wasn't ... I don't ...' she

spluttered, appalled by what he had just said
about her, denials tumbling out of her furiously as
she glared at his mocking face through a red haze
of outrage. 'I don't know how you can accuse me
of being what you say I am. You didn't have to
pull me down beside you on to the sand. You
didn't have to kiss me or ... or touch me,' she
went on more coherently in a low, angry voice.

'No, I didn't have to. And maybe that's why I
stopped when I realised what you were doing,' he
retorted through tight lips. 'You're a cheat, Stella,
and I don't much care for cheats. You're going to
marry Brian, yet this afternoon you wanted me to
make love to you. That's cheating.' He drew his
right hand from the pocket of his shorts and
dangled the keys of the truck before her. 'You
might give these to Harriet, when you see her and
thank her for the use of the truck,' he added
coolly.

She took the keys from him without a word and
standing as if turned to stone, stunned by his last
accusation she watched him walk away through the
trees.

CHAPTER FIVE

'So you're back at last.' Harriet appeared at one of the open glass doors and slid back the screen. 'Where's Kit?'

'Gone to the dive-ship, I suppose. He asked me to give you these.' Stella handed the truck keys over.

'My goodness, you're very pale. I hope you didn't feel travel-sick in the truck,' said Harriet stepping back into the lounge to let Stella pass inside. 'I know the road between here and the village is rough.'

'No. I wasn't travel-sick. I just feel a little tired, that's all.'

'Then come and have a drink. On the house of course,' said Harriet hospitably. 'We're all having one. We have some guests for the evening. They came in on a yacht and it's docked down at the jetty.'

Stella glanced over at the bar and the people clustered about it, both men and women all dressed in sailing clothes.

'No, not just now,' she started to say when Brian detached himself from the group and came over to her, smiling.

'Did you get through to Audrey?' he asked.

'Yes. No problem.' She glanced at the glass in his hand. 'Not like you to drink hard liquor,' she murmured.

'I'm drowning my sorrows,' he said lightly. 'About not finding anything in the crevasse. Come and have one too. What would you like?'

'What are you having?'

'Harriet's variation on a Planter's Punch. It's mostly fruit juices with a little rum. Won't do you any harm or interfere with your diving,' he said. 'Harriet, another of these for Stella,' he called out. 'Sit down,' he went on, turning back to Stella and pushing forward one of the bar stools. 'You seem shaken up.'

'It was the ride in the truck. The road is really rough.' She slid on to the stool and looked over to the other side of the curved bar counter. The man who was sitting there seemed to be staring at her intently. Black-haired and black-bearded he seemed familiar to her but she couldn't quite place him. In the next instant she had dismissed the possibility that she knew him. Beards and moustaches tended to make dark-haired men all look alike.

'What's the village like?' asked Brian.

'I thought you'd been there,' she said in surprise. 'I thought you stayed with Harriet and Larry two years ago?'

'I never went to the village, though. I spent most of my time here, underwater with Larry.'

'It's just a cluster of houses, a church and a hotel, a dock for the mail-boat and any freighters that call. The people are friendly, though. Everyone waved to us as we passed.'

'Here you are, Stella. Your Planter's Punch,' said Harriet setting down a tall glass full of a pinkish liquid decorated with a slice of lime. 'Like another, Brian?'

'No, thanks.'

'You'll have to excuse me,' said Harriet. 'The others want more drinks and until Charlie, the barman, comes, I guess I'm barman.'

'You should be more strict with your employees,'

said Brian. 'Dismiss them if they can't come to work on time.'

'Dismiss an islander?' Harriet's large teeth glittered as she laughed. 'Oh, we can't do that. Once they're in our employment they're with us for ever. Anyway, I wouldn't want to dismiss any of them. I love them all. They're instead of children. Charlie will turn up sooner or later, you'll see. And I couldn't possibly sack him. He makes the best piña coladas in the Caribbean.' One of the screens slid open and a young black man smartly dressed in dark trousers and a crisp white shirt stepped in. 'Here he is,' crowed Harriet. 'Hi, Charlie.'

'Sorry I'm late, Missus Harriet, ma'am,' he said, grinning all over his face. 'My bicycle had a puncture and I had to push the stupid thing all the way here. Now what you doin' back there, ma'am? Tryin' to take my job over?'

He slid behind the bar and Harriet turned away to talk to him privately. Stella sipped some of the drink through the straw provided, glad she didn't have to pick up the glass. She was still dithery after her emotional clash with Kit and wanted nothing more than to go to her room, fling herself down on the bed and cry. As she finished sipping she looked over at the man with the black beard. He was still staring at her. She turned to Brian, worried by that stare. Supposing he was someone she knew or had met and come over to speak to her, she would be embarrassed because she didn't recognise him.

'Brian, when you went diving two years ago with Professor Lundgren was it then he found the artefacts that have been identified as having belonged to the *Santiago*?' she asked.

He gave her a puzzled glance and ruffled his hair.

'No, no,' he said with a touch of impatience. 'You should remember because I told you Larry found the treas— I mean those valuables when he was diving alone last year. It was after he had been to Spain to have them identified that he came to me at the university and suggested that the site be registered and explored for the remains of the galleon, and we made application to the government of the islands for permission to explore and to take any artefacts back to Britain to be examined.'

'Then when you were here you didn't explore the crevasse or the rest of the reef?'

'Yes, as a matter of fact we did dive near that particular reef,' he replied with a little laugh. 'Nothing there, except fish. Why all the questions?'

'I . . .' She took another sip of her drink quickly, wondering how she was going to bring up the matter of the wreck lying under the outgrowth of coral on the other side of the reef from the crevasse. 'Did you look through Larry's notes this afternoon?' she asked quickly, changing her mind about what she had intended to say.

'Yes, I did.' He shook his head slowly from side to side. 'I hadn't missed anything. I didn't think I had.'

'I didn't think we had either,' she admitted. 'But I just wondered whether you'd come across any reference to . . .'

'Excuse me,' interrupted a voice with a drawling accent much like Kit's, 'but haven't I met you before?'

Stella swung round on her stool. What she had hoped wouldn't happen had happened. The man with the beard was standing beside her, looking at her with merry brown eyes, and looking into those eyes she recognised him at once. He was Bob Dawson, a friend of Kit's who worked as a charter captain, skippering a forty-two foot ketch out of a charter fleet based in St Thomas.

'I . . . I don't think so,' she said weakly, aware that Harriet had come from behind the bar and perched on a stool beside Brian and was listening.

'Well, if I haven't, I beg your pardon,' he said pleasantly. 'But you're the spitting image of a woman I met a few years ago. She was English, too, but I can't remember her name offhand. She was on a yacht that was cruising around the islands.'

'I suppose I'm just a typical English type,' said Stella with a light laugh. 'There are probably replicas of me all over the world.' She half turned away from him to sip some more of her drink. She was beginning to shake again and was relieved when one of the charter party called to Bob Dawson to ask if she could go back to the yacht to get something.

'Well, sorry I've bothered you,' he said. 'The name is Bob Dawson, by the way. Does that ring any bells with you?'

'No, I'm afraid not.' Stella didn't turn to him again although she guessed he thought she was rude for not telling him her name.

'Her name is Stella. Stella Grayson. Does that ring any bells with you, Bob?' asked Harriet brightly and Stella stiffened all over.

'Bob,' called a whining female voice. 'Come on. Come with me to the yacht. You know I can't get aboard without help.'

''Scuse me, right now,' said Bob. 'I'll see you again. You're staying here, Stella?'

'Yes, she's staying here,' said Harriet and he went off through one of the doors with a small dark woman who had the whining voice.

'Funny that he thinks he's met you before,' said Harriet. 'And in these islands too. I thought you told me you'd only been to Nassau.'

'Have you, Stella? I didn't know that,' exclaimed Brian. 'When were you in Nassau?'

'Oh, about four years ago. I stayed with an old school friend who had married a Bahamian.' She pressed the back of her hand against her forehead. Her skin was damp with sweat and she felt strangely exhausted, physically and emotionally drained. Deceit had never come easily to her and now she was beginning to wish she hadn't decided to pretend she had never met Kit before. It would have been better if she had told Brian the truth from the beginning. 'Brian, do you think we could go somewhere to talk ... alone,' she whispered, glancing at Harriet, who had turned away to talk to one of the guests. 'There's something I have to tell you. About the wreck site,' she added quickly when she saw him frown hesitantly.

'I suppose we could go for a walk. Or sit on the terrace outside your room or mine,' he said slowly.

'Don't you ever want to be alone with me?' she chided him lightly, thinking how unloverlike he was, wondering if he would ever catch her up in his arms. Or pull her down beside him as Kit had done that afternoon ... Ah, no, no, she must forget the sudden savagery of Kit's love-making that afternoon. It hadn't been love-making. It had been more like a punishment, a punishment for wanting him when she was engaged to be married to Brian.

'Of course I do,' said Brian, but he sounded diffident.

'Then let's go now to my room terrace.' She slipped off the stool. 'It's so noisy in here now. We can't hear ourselves speak.'

'All right. You go ahead and I'll follow you in a few seconds. I'll just tell Harriet . . .'

'Why? Why do you have to tell her?' she demanded swinging back to him.

'She might wonder where we've gone.'

Stella didn't wait. She turned on her heel, went to one of the sliding screen doors, slammed it open, stepped outside and slammed it shut. The slamming relieved her feelings a little but she was still irritated by Brian's lack of urgent desire to be alone with her. Why did he want to marry her if he didn't want to be with her? And why did he have to tell Harriet where he was going? Did the woman have some hold over him? Was it possible he and Harriet were partners together in some sort of conspiracy to hunt for treasure as Kit had suggested?

She marched down the steps from the terrace and along the path through the trees. The sun was setting, streaking the western sky with rainbow colours, glowing fierily behind the black silhouettes of the trees. Insects sang in the undergrowth and a few nibbled at her bare arms and legs. The wind had died down and where the sun was setting a planet had appeared in the sky, a bright star blazing brilliantly with white fire.

Then suddenly the serene silence was shattered by a commotion of voices on the terrace behind her. Deciding that the charter party and the other guests had spilled noisily out of the bar on to the terrace she continued on her way wondering when Brian would catch up with her. A few seconds he had said he would be. Had Harriet prevented him from joining her? She wouldn't be at all surprised if the woman had coaxed him into staying in the lounge, maybe with another offer of a 'drink on the house'.

But she didn't care, she realised. She didn't care if Brian didn't follow her or if he preferred Harriet's company and another Planter's Punch to herself . . .

'Stella. Stella. Come back. Come now. Brian's had an accident.' Harriet's voice was shrill and penetrating, carrying through the purple, rose-shot gloom.

Oh, God, what now? Why couldn't she get away from them, have some time to herself to reflect, to try and unravel the tangled web that had been spun about her ever since she had arrived on the island four days ago?

'Stella.' Harriet came surging out of the shadows. 'Come back. Brian sent me to fetch you. To tell you he can't follow you.' She paused to catch her breath then went on in a lower acid-toned voice 'Yes, he sent me to get you. As if you cared for him. As if you'll worry because he's hurt himself.'

'What has he done?' exclaimed Stella, starting off along the path, back the way she had come. Harriet panted beside her.

'Oh, he was following you, running after you. Why couldn't you have waited for him? He was running down the terrace steps and fell. I think he may have twisted his ankle. Fortunately one of the sports fishermen is a doctor. Oh, it's all your fault,' hissed Harriet. 'You should have waited for him. You're not fit to be his wife. You're too young, too thoughtless. Brian needs someone to coddle him, wait on him.'

'Someone like you, I suppose,' said Stella drily.

'Right. Someone like me,' asserted Harriet and bounced up the terrace steps.

In the lounge Brian was lying on one of the sofas, both legs straight out before him. A dark-haired, thick-set man was sitting beside him, talking to him.

'A damned silly thing to do,' said Brian smiling up at Stella when she approached the sofa. His usually pale face was even paler and the bluish smudges under his eyes looked black.

'I'm so sorry,' she said, crouching down beside the sofa and looking at his bare left foot. There was a swelling coming up below the ankle bone and the skin was discoloured. 'Is the pain very bad?'

'I've given him a couple of pain-killers,' said the other man. 'Not much you can do for a sprain except rest it.' He patted Brian on the shoulder and stood up. 'No more diving for you, feller, for a couple of weeks. Stay on dry land. You'll need some crutches so you can hop about.'

The doctor, after nodding at Stella, wandered back to his friends at the bar.

'Will we be able to get crutches here on the island?'

'I can get in touch with the island doctor by radio,' said Harriet. 'I'll ask him to come out tomorrow to look at your ankle, Brian. He will probably have some crutches.'

'Are you sure you wouldn't like to be flown to St Thomas to the hospital there and get another opinion,' suggested Stella.

To her annoyance he looked past her and up at Harriet as if seeking some advice. 'No. I'll be all right. I'll stay here.' He attempted a smile. 'After

all, we are supposed to be on holiday. Now we can
really rest for a while.'

'But what about the exploration?' asked Stella,
settling more comfortably on the floor beside the
sofa. 'Don't you want me to continue the search in
the crevasse?'

He frowned and shifted about on the sofa as if
trying to find a more comfortable position.

'I don't like the idea of you diving alone under
that freighter,' he murmured.

'Gerry or Kit could dive with me.'

'Mmm. I suppose so. We'll have to discuss it
with Harriet. I don't suppose she'll object to Gerry
but . . .' He broke off, glanced about him, then
leaned towards her and added in a low voice, 'To
tell the truth neither Harriet nor I trust Barlow. If
Cowan were here it would be different.'

'He'll be here soon,' she comforted him. 'He'll
come tomorrow, perhaps. Kit phoned him this
afternoon.' She paused, studied his pale face for a
moment, then asked, 'Why don't you like Kit?
You personally, I mean.'

'Oh, I don't dislike him,' he hedged uncomfortably. 'I just feel that he isn't exactly on our
side. He's been very critical of my persistence in
searching in the crevasse, seems to think that
Larry made a mistake in saying that it's the site of
the wreck of the *Santiago*. He isn't the sort of
person we would want to share in any discovery
we might make.'

'You mean you wouldn't want him to share in
the treasure you're hoping to find?' suggested
Stella quietly, watching him from beneath her
eyelids. She thought his mouth tightened and that
the quick glance he gave her was somewhat wary.

'Well, hardly treasure,' he said. 'Only what you or

I would call treasure, historical artefacts from which we might be able to piece together a description of the way of life on a Spanish colonial ship, what sort of people travelled on such ships, what luggage they carried with them and so on.'

'You're not expecting to find much in the way of silver or gold or jewellery then?'

'How could we find any more than has already been found? Have you forgotten it's a ship that had been looted we're looking for?' he remarked rather sharply.

'Well, I hope you'll agree to me diving again tomorrow morning with Gerry as a companion. I'd like to go round to the other side of the reef and explore there.'

'Why?' The questions seemed to explode from him. He had raised his head from the cushion against which he had been resting and was staring at her, eyes wide and watchful. 'Why do you want to explore there?'

'Just to see if there are any remains of a wreck there.' She had decided that in view of what he had said about Kit it would be wiser not to mention that Kit had been exploring on his own and had found a wooden ship wedged under the coral on the other side of the reef from the crevasse.

'You won't find anything there. Larry and I searched that side thoroughly when we dived at the reef a couple of years ago,' he said. 'Don't waste your time, Stella, looking around there. I'd rather you didn't go diving without me. I'd much prefer you to wait until Jack Cowan is here. Besides I'd like your company while I have to loaf about resting this ankle.'

'Would you really?' she asked, giving him a penetrating glance.

'Of course I would. Why, do you doubt it?'
Much to her surprise he reached out and took
hold of one of her hands, an unusual de-
monstration of affection on his part.

'Yes, I do sometimes. You didn't seem over-
eager to be alone with me when I asked if we
might talk together privately,' she murmured.

'I'm sorry if I gave you that impression,' he said.
'I didn't intend to. What was it you wanted to talk
about? Something to do with the wreck site, I
think you said.'

She had said that to him thinking it would
tempt him to go with her at the time but she had
really intended to tell him about having met and
known Kit before this visit to Sanada. Now she
hesitated about telling him in a room where there
were other people. It would have to wait again for
a more suitable occasion, perhaps the next day
when she was keeping him company while he was
'loafing about'.

'I was only going to ask you if Professor
Lundgren had mentioned finding any other
artefacts, perhaps on the other side of the reef,' she
murmured. 'But you've answered that already ...'
Her words trailed off into silence because he had
obviously lost interest and was looking past her at
someone coming towards them. Harriet of course.

'I hope you two have had that little talk you
wanted to have,' Harriet said, 'shared all your
secrets with each other.' She smiled sweetly,
looking from Stella to Brian and then back to
Stella again. 'Dinner is ready now. Can we help
you into the dining-room, Brian?'

'I think I can hop over there,' he said, swinging
his legs off the sofa and standing up on one foot
while his other was held a few inches off the floor.

'I'm just going to wash my hands and tidy up a little, first,' said Stella. 'I'll be back in a few minutes.'

Brian nodded and she turned away almost colliding with the dark woman with the whining voice who had returned from the charter yacht. The woman was alone. Bob Dawson hadn't come with her.

'Oh, Harriet,' Stella heard the woman say. 'Captain Bob says please will you excuse him. He won't be having dinner with us. He's met an old friend of his, the skipper of the dive-ship and he'll be having dinner with him on the ship.'

So Bob had met Kit again, thought Stella as she stepped out on to the terrace again and made for the steps. By now it must have dawned on Bob who she was, and where and with whom she had been when he had met her. Would he come back later to the resort and confront her, announce for everyone to hear that he had met her in St Thomas and at the time she had been living with Kit Barlow on his yacht? In that case she had better tell Brian about Kit and herself before Bob reappeared.

She let herself into her room recalling Kit's bitter accusation that she was a cheat. How she wished that she had never suggested to him that they pretend they had never met. Why had she done it? To protect Brian from being hurt by the truth. Because Brian wouldn't understand, she had told Kit. But if Brian loved her he wouldn't give a damn about what she had done four years ago. She didn't give a damn about his past. It didn't matter to her that he had been married and divorced. She wasn't jealous of his ex-wife. So why should knowing that she had an affair before she had met him upset him?

You're a cheat, Stella, and I don't much care for cheats. How those sneering words of Kit's had sliced through to her heart. They had hurt her far more than anything Brian might say to her, she realised.

She sank down on the edge of the bed with a groan. Oh, what had she done? What *had* she done? In asking Kit to go along with her in the pretence of not knowing him and never having met him she had forfeited his good opinion of her and lost any respect he had still felt for her by seeking a few moments of pleasure with him this afternoon.

Which mattered to her the most? Kit's respect or Brian's? Whose love did she want the most? Kit's. The answer came up from the depths of her feelings unhesitatingly and she groaned again because she wasn't sure he loved her. He wouldn't have let her leave him in Nassau, if he had loved her. He wouldn't have thrust her away from him so angrily this afternoon if he loved her.

She washed, changed her clothes and returned to the dining-room resolved to tell Brian the truth about herself and Kit as soon as the opportunity presented itself, while they were having dinner, if possible, before Bob Dawson reappeared. Harriet was sitting at the table with Brian, leaning towards him confidentially as she talked. Stella sat opposite to him. He already had a plateful of food, served by Harriet, no doubt.

'I hear you're willing to go diving again tomorrow by yourself,' Harriet said.

'Not by myself. I'll take Gerry with me.'

'I think I might come out on the dive-ship with you,' said Harriet. 'Everyone is leaving early in the morning and there'll be no guests coming in.' She turned to smile at Brian. 'You won't mind us going off together without you, will you? Eulalie, the housekeeper, will look after you, bring you anything you want.'

'I'd rather Stella didn't dive without me,' Brian replied frowning. 'Much better to wait for Jack Cowan to come.'

'If he comes,' said Harriet. 'How do we know Kit Barlow isn't lying about that, too? Besides I don't want to be paying out for that ship to lie idle at the jetty.' She smiled at Stella. 'Do go and help yourself as usual from the buffet, Stella. Remember, no one is going to bring food to you. Only Brian gets special treatment while he can't walk about without pain.'

Taking the hint, Stella rose to her feet and went to the long table where the food was set out and helped herself to a slice of roast beef, some potato salad, a slice of corn bread and some tomato salad. When she returned to her place Harriet bounded to her feet and went over to another table to lean over her guests and make sure they were comfortable and all had what they needed.

She overdoes it, thought Stella as she picked at her food. She's much too hearty and I loathe the way she touches people on the shoulder, breathes down their necks, overwhelms them with attention . . .

'Harriet has just been remarking again how strange it was when that charter skipper thought he recognised you. Seems he knows Barlow, too,' Brian's voice broke into her thoughts and she glanced away from the shoulder-caressing Harriet to him. He was staring at her from under frowning eyebrows. 'How long did you stay in Nassau with your friend?'

'With Shirley? Oh, about three weeks.' she replied casually, but felt herself go tense. Was the moment of truth closer than she had thought?

'And where did you go after that?'

'Where?' She was puzzled by the question.

'Yes. Where? You didn't return to England, to the university. You didn't return there until the following October. I know you took a leave of absence.' He smiled slightly. 'A letter that came to the department soon after I'd taken over that January four years ago was from you. In it you wrote to say you would be absent for a few months and hoped you would be allowed to return the next autumn to continue your studies towards a master's degree. I remember consulting Davison, about you. He thought so highly of your work that he advised me to let you back into the department when you returned because he thought I might find you useful in the undersea explorations. So I kept a place open for you. But in the letter you didn't say where you were going or what you would be doing while you were away.'

'You could always have asked me where I'd been and what I'd been doing when I returned,' she pointed out.

'Yes, I suppose I could. It just didn't occur to me at the time. I've always tried to treat my students with respect for their personal lives. I've always preferred not to enquire into their private business.'

'We have noticed,' she said. 'And have appreciated your professional attitude.'

'But the situation is different now, between you and me, Stella. You are no longer just a student of mine. You're an assistant lecturer in the department, a professional colleague and you are also

going to be my wife. As a colleague, I wouldn't
expect you to tell me where you went and what
you did during that leave of absence but as the
person you are going to marry I am interested in
anything you have done and would like to know
more about you.'

How dry he was. As dry as dust, Kit had said.
Dry, cold but indirect, going round a subject,
explaining all the time, giving the historical
background to his question. And how different
from Kit.

'It is still my private business,' she murmured,
playing for time and heard him sigh.

'You don't want to tell me,' he accused quietly.
'You don't want to tell me because you're
ashamed of what you did and where you went.'

She glanced up at him quickly. Had she been
forestalled by Harriet after all? Had Harriet
overheard what she and Kit had said to each other
by the jetty on Monday night?

'Ashamed?' she exclaimed angrily, but kept her
voice as quiet as his. 'No. Never ashamed. I did
what I did and went where I went because I
wanted to. I also did it for love.'

'Love?' He was startled.

'Yes, love. I would guess that is something you
don't know much about, Brian.'

'Stella, this isn't the place or time to discuss our
emotions,' he muttered sending sidelong glances at
the other tables. 'All I did was ask a simple
question.'

'About my past. If you loved me you wouldn't
want to know about it. All right, I'll answer your
question to show you I'm not ashamed of anything
I've done. During those months I "goofed off".
Know what that means?'

'Er, yes. I think so. You escaped from your responsibilities.' There was a note of censure in his voice and he looked like the severe and very critical teacher that he was.

'That's right. I forgot all my responsibilities and my ambition. I went cruising with a man on his yacht. I had a wonderful time and incidentally I learned to dive. Those nine months were the best months of my life to date and I'll never forget them. Or him,' she finished defiantly.

'Just the two of you on his yacht,' said Brian tonelessly.

'Just the two of us. Can you believe it of me?'

'I don't want to believe it,' he said sullenly. 'I don't want to.'

'You knew before you asked me that question, didn't you?' she accused. 'Harriet told you. Well, now you know the truth, Brian, about me and Kit.' She rose to her feet. 'I'm going to bed now. I'm tired and I'd like to be up and off early to go diving. I'll just have a word with Harriet on my way out. Good night.'

'Stella. Wait.' He struggled to his feet, wincing as he forgot about his injured ankle. 'Stella, I'd like you to know that knowing the truth doesn't make any difference. I still want to marry you,' he whispered desperately.

She went back to him, her attitude softening. Smiling, she kissed him on the cheek.

'We'll talk about that tomorrow, shall we?' she said softly. 'I hope you have a good night and not too much pain.'

'Going to bed already, Stella?' Harriet had emerged from the kitchen.

'Yes. What time would you like to go on the ship to the reef?'

'The earlier the better for me,' said Harriet. 'Could we leave around eight thirty?'

'Fine with me, but we'll have to send a message to the ship.'

'I'll send Charlie down later.'

'Good. Oh, by the way, Harriet, I've told Brian about the holiday I took four years ago, cruising among the islands, after I left Nassau. He'll probably tell you about it and you can fill in the details. 'Night.'

Leaving by way of the terrace Stella sprang down the steps. She felt wonderful, as free as air. The load was off her mind. Brian knew about her affair with Kit and he still wanted to marry her. Now all she had to do was tell Kit that she didn't have to pretend she hadn't met him before and maybe she would win back his respect. She would have gone now to tell him, but Bob would be with him and, anyway, to visit him on board ship even if Bob wasn't with him would be too risky. She might find herself wanting him to make love to her so she mustn't place herself in that position. She didn't want to hear him calling her a cheat ever again.

CHAPTER SIX

THE next morning was cool and tranquil, the best part of the day in the tropics, Stella thought, as she made her way with Harriet along the path through the trees to the jetty, when everything was fresh and clear after a good night's rest. Emerald and turquoise, the water gleamed, satin smooth, in the bay. On land the fringed fronds of the palms seemed as if they had been newly washed and the delicate petals of oleander blossoms edging the pathway looked as if their tints had just been touched up by an artist with his brush.

Yet Harriet's mood was anything but tranquil, Stella guessed, glancing sideways at her companion. Dressed in white slacks with a loose pink shirt, Harriet was walking along in sullen silence, her sunglasses hiding her eyes but not the fierce scowl of her finely plucked eyebrows or the set of her square jaw.

'Look, Harriet, if you would rather not come . . .' Stella began, only to be interrupted roughly.

'Who said anything about me not wanting to come?' Harriet demanded tautly. 'I have to come. Someone in authority has to be on board while Brian is out of action to keep an eye on that arrogant bastard.'

'I suppose you're referring to Kit Barlow,' said Stella.

'You're darned right I am.'

'I thought you liked him, found him attractive,' Stella couldn't help teasing.

'Not any more. Not since I've found out how untrustworthy he is. He's been diving, while you and Brian have been underwater, poking about where he has no right, on the other side of the reef.'

'How do you know he has?' exclaimed Stella. 'Did he tell you?'

'No. Gerry told us. Yesterday afternoon. I'm not having him diving where he has no right to dive today. I'm going to make quite sure he stays on board.'

'But there's nothing to stop me or Gerry from going over to the other side of the reef and poking about too,' argued Stella. 'Once we're underwater you'll have no idea where we are. And the water is free, you know.'

'The wrecks aren't. Nor are the sites of wrecks,' retorted Harriet stubbornly. 'You have to have permission from the government of these islands to dive and we have permission to examine only the site that Larry discovered. If Kit Barlow goes diving again today against my orders I'm going to report him to the government. If I let him go on behaving as he is doing without attempting to restrain him we might lose our permission to explore . . .'

'I don't believe you would,' said Stella. 'The government has no way of policing the underwater areas. And I haven't seen any sign of a coastguard or a security patrol in this bay or near the reef.'

'That's because I haven't reported him yet,' snapped Harriet. 'But I will if he doesn't do what I say. I'll make damned sure he loses his diver's licence.'

'Oh, this is really silly,' protested Stella. 'For all you know Kit might find the *Santiago* for you.

He's an excellent diver and explorer, will go into dangerous places without turning a hair . . .'

'Oh, yes. You should know. You lived with him for nearly a year, didn't you?' sneered Harriet. 'You must know all about him.'

'Brian told you then about my having cruised about the islands with Kit,' said Stella quietly.

'About your affair with him? He told me you'd confessed at last to having met Barlow four years ago. But I knew you'd had an affair with him. I heard you and him talking the first night he was here. Who do you think suggested to Brian that he ask you where you'd been and what you'd done during that year. Me.' Harriet laughed scornfully. 'Bob Dawson really scared you last night, didn't he? I thought somehow you'd be telling the truth to Brian before the day was over.'

'I'm glad now I've told him. It hasn't made any difference between us. We're still going to be married when this expedition is over,' replied Stella coolly, and stepping on to the jetty she strode ahead of Harriet towards the gangway of the *Sea Urchin*, noticing as she did that the charter yacht captained by Bob Dawson had gone and so had the sports fishermen's powerboat.

When she and Harriet stepped aboard the dive-ship Kit was there to greet them.

'Good morning,' he said smoothly. 'Nice to have you aboard, Harriet. Sorry to hear about the professor's ankle. You're sure you want to dive without him, Stella?'

'Gerry can keep me company,' she replied. Actually she was bursting to tell him there and then that she had told Brian the truth about their brief affair and that it made no difference, she was still going to marry Brian, but she couldn't with

Harriet and Gerry standing by. It would have to wait until she could be alone with him.

'We would like to leave right away,' asserted Harriet bossily. 'I can't afford to have you or this ship idle at a thousand dollars a day.'

'Of course not,' murmured Kit, still suave although Stella thought she detected a glint of anger in his eyes before he turned away to give orders to Gerry and Matt to cast off the warps. 'Perhaps you'd like to steer the ship, Harriet,' she heard him say, and he escorted the other woman up the companionway to the wheelhouse.

The ship was under way sliding through the smooth sunlit water, and Stella was on the foredeck enjoying as always the view of sea and land: the golden gleam of sand backed by the various greens of vegetation, the silvery jade green of shallow water close to the shore, the deeper almost purple shade nearer the horizon, the sight of pelicans in flight formation, swooping low over the water, hustling the fish they could see below the surface, when she became aware that someone was standing beside her, leaning on the rail too. She turned her head. Kit was beside her, tanned and lithe, his elbow just touching hers and immediately but unexpectedly she was swamped with all kinds of tingling sensations, her body's instinctive response to his powerful masculinity, something which never happened to her when she was with Brian. Nor when she was with any other man for that matter, she thought ruefully. Only Kit, it seemed, could awaken feelings of passionate desire within her, could kindle the naked flame that scorched through her.

'Who is steering? Harriet?' she asked, uneasily glancing at the wheelhouse.

'No. The auto-pilot. Gerry is keeping an eye on it. She is talking to him. Giving him orders.' His lip curled cynically. 'Did you know she and Brian commandeered the ship yesterday afternoon and went out to the reef?'

'No. Why did they do that? Did Gerry and Matt go with them?'

'They did.' He grinned wryly. 'Matt was most apologetic when he told me. It seems that Harriet really threw her weight about, insisting that she was in command of the expeditions since she was paying for the hire of the ship and its crew and that they'd better do what she said or else she'd make damned sure they lost their jobs. She also got Gerry to admit that I'd been diving on the other side of the reef.' He turned to give her a slow appraising glance. 'Did you tell Brian what I told you about the wreck that is wedged under the coral?'

'No, I didn't. I decided not to. I wonder why he didn't tell me he and Harriet went out to the reef again? I thought he thought it was too windy, that there was too much surge for us to dive yesterday afternoon. Did he dive?'

'Yes. Alone. Said he had had a sudden idea and wanted to check it out. The surge wasn't too bad, apparently.' He considered her again thoughtfully, his eyes slitted against the bright light. 'So he didn't tell you?' he murmured.

'No. Nor did Harriet. And when I suggested that I explore the other side of the reef this morning, he told me it would be a waste of time because he and Professor Lundgren explored there two years ago and found nothing.'

'Or found the wreck I saw and didn't want anyone else to know about it,' remarked Kit drily.

'I'll dive with you this morning, show you where it is and we'll see if we can get inside it.'

'But Harriet has come to make sure you don't dive,' she exclaimed.

'I don't really see how she can stop me,' he drawled. 'Do you?'

'She says she'll report you to the government of the islands and also the authority which issued your diving licence.'

'So what?' He shrugged. 'I'll report her and Haines for piracy.'

'Piracy? But what evidence have you got? What have they stolen?'

'Wait until you've been with me to that wreck,' he murmured leaning his head close to hers, his hair touching hers, his lips very close to her cheek. 'I bet seeing Bob Dawson shook you up.'

'Oh, it did.' She moved a little along the rail away from him, sending a quick glance up at the wheelhouse. When he came after her and leaned close to her again she whispered, 'Kit, please don't come so near. Harriet is watching.'

'Let her watch.' He rubbed his cheeks against hers. 'You smell good in the morning, Stella. I bet you taste good, too.' His lips nibbled her cheek.

'I . . . you . . . told me yesterday that you didn't care for cheats,' she pointed out as he put an arm around her waist.

'I know I did. That was how I felt yesterday about you. Today I feel differently. I realised in the night that I only pushed you away from me yesterday afternoon on account of the poor old professor. But why should I deny myself some pleasure if you're willing? Why should I worry about him being cheated when you obviously don't care a hang whether you cheat him or not?'

His voice soft and deep had an unpleasant undercurrent of contempt.

'Wait, wait. Listen to me, please.' She pushed his hand away from her waist and while facing him backed away from him. 'Last night I told Brian that I had met you before and that I spent some time cruising with you. I told him because well, because I was finding pretending too much of a strain and also, I suppose, because I couldn't have Bob Dawson coming back and saying that he had remembered where he had met me before after he had seen you yesterday evening. He did remember me when he saw you, didn't he?'

'He sure did. That was why I kept him with me for the rest of the evening. I warned him you wouldn't like it if he spilled the beans about you and me in front of Haines and Harriet.' He stepped close to her again. In the breeze created by the passage of the ship his sun-streaked hair lifted and his eyes were blue flames. 'So you came clean with Haines. Was he upset, as you expected?'

'Not as much as I had expected. He said it wouldn't change anything, wouldn't change how he feels about me. We're still going to be married when we return to England.'

'I see.' The words hissed softly between his teeth. No longer ablaze with desire, his eyes were icy.

'Now you and I won't have to pretend we don't know each other,' she went on.

'Then let's celebrate, shall we?' Too quick for her he scooped her into his arms and kissed her hard and thoroughly. Unprepared for such an attack her lips responded to the rough rather contemptuous pressure of his. Her hands clutching his arms to push him away and yet to hold him at the same time, she kissed him back vigorously, giving in to her frustrated desire to be close to him and make love with him.

'But just because Brian knows about us doesn't mean to say we should behave as if we're still intimate,' she remonstrated when Kit lifted his lips from hers. 'Until you pointed it out to me I didn't realise I was cheating on Brian when we were on the beach. You see, I was so glad to be with you away from the others, away from being watched that I forgot about my promise to marry him.'

His arms fell away from her and his upper lip curled in a sneer. 'You're really something else, Stella. You're going to marry him yet you forgot about him yesterday afternoon. You kiss me, offer me the freedom of your body but you're still going to marry him.' Every word he spoke seemed to sting like a hailstone. 'I've heard about women like you,' he continued. 'You can't find everything you want in one man so you have to have two: one for the entertainment of your mind, the other for the gratification of your senses . . .'

'No. That isn't true. I'm not like that,' she began to argue when her attention was caught by a movement behind him. Harriet was coming down the companionway from the wheelhouse. 'I can't discuss this with you any longer,' she went on in a lower voice. 'Harriet is coming this way. When will you dive with me?'

'You and Gerry go down together to the crevasse. When you come up for your second tank of air I'll go over the side from the bow while Harriet is busy talking to you and Gerry on the afterdeck. I'll meet you at the crevasse. Gerry will stay on board,' he said, coolly authoritative now.

'But won't Harriet give him a bad time if he doesn't dive with me?'

'He knows what to do if she does,' he replied
tersely. 'Go and get ready to dive now. I'll deal
with Harriet. She looks as if she might burst a
blood vessel at any minute.'

He strolled towards Harriet, hands in the
pockets of his shorts, and as she made her escape
along the side deck Stella could hear him speaking
pleasantly to the other woman, soothing her. The
engines were slowing down. They were entering
the cove so she hurried into one of the small cabins
to change into a one-piece swimsuit, deciding that
it would be too warm for a wetsuit.

She and Gerry had no problems getting into the
water. As always under the surface—unless there
was a surge—it was peaceful and far away from
the turbulence of personal relationships, thought
Stella as she drifted downwards into a world of
blue light among shoals of indifferent fish. For
half an hour, as long as they had air in their tanks,
she and Gerry worked, each of them clearing away
debris and sand from the section of the old buried
timbers allotted to them by Brian, sifting through
the sand and coral carefully hoping to find a shard
of pottery or a piece of metal that might give them
information about the wreck beneath them.

She had just checked her air-meter when she heard
Gerry give a muffled shout. Turning she saw him
waving to her excitedly and pointing to a cavity in
the timbers he had cleared. In his other hand he held
an oval iron ball that fitted comfortably into the
palm of his hand. Looking into the hole at which he
was pointing she saw several other oval shapes. She
picked one out and indicated that she was going up.
He nodded and they made their ascent together.
Both Harriet and Matt were on the afterdeck,
waiting to help them change their tanks.

'But whatever are they?' asked Harriet when they showed her their finds.

'Weapons of some sort,' said Gerry who was excited by the find. 'Now we're beginning to get somewhere. I don't know about you guys but I'd nearly given up, thinking we'd never find anything that might be Spanish. Those are Spanish, aren't they, Stella?'

'Yes, I believe so. They're the wrong shape for musket shot and too big, but too small for cannon,' she replied thoughtfully. 'They're probably hand grenades. This piece of wood attached to the end would be the fuse. The Spaniards invented them you know and they take their name from *granadas*, Spanish for the pomegranate fruit which they resemble. I'm going down again to get some more.'

A fresh air-tank on her back, mask over her eyes and mouthpiece of her air-tube in her mouth, she walked off the ladder into the water and sank immediately, pulled down by the weights at her waist. Soon she was at the entrance to the crevasse. A long shadowy figure appeared. Kit was there as he had promised, and together they swam along the formidable wall of coral that was the dangerous reef. When they reached the end of it they turned into a wide bay and floated down further to an overhanging growth of coral near which a barracuda hung motionless, big-jawed and glassy-eyed, challenging them to move another inch.

Kit indicated to her that she should hang, too, in the water like the fish and stare back at it. The tactic worked. After a while the barracuda backed off rather disdainfully much to Stella's relief. She knew that barracudas don't attack divers but she never could be sure that the fish knew it. As soon as it had gone Kit beckoned to her to follow him under the overhanging growth of coral. Soon she was staring not at a barracuda but in amazement at the after part of the hull of a wooden ship. Holes gaped between the worm-eaten, coral-encrusted timbers and many fish—she recognised parrot fish, angel fish and yellow snappers—swam in and out of the hull. At the stern where the rudder was still attached numerous clumps of colourful orange-cup corals thrived in the relative darkness.

Following Kit she floated upwards and over the edge of the hull which was lying at a forty-degree angle on firm sand. Inside was a shambles of broken timbers. Obeying Kit's come-on signal she followed him to a section of the hull that had been cleared by some previous visitors. There in a cavity was what appeared to be an iron chest. She swam closer to it. It wasn't iron at all. It was a simple, cheap, tin chest, the sort that students often use to pack all their goods and chattels in when they are on the move, quite modern in design, and it was padlocked.

She looked at Kit enquiringly. He indicated something that must be 'the treasure' and pointed to his air-meter showing that their time below was running out and they should go back to the dive-ship. On her way out of the wreck she searched, out of habit, for artefacts and picked up from the sand some darkened discs which could have been silver coins, part of a pottery jar made from rough clay, and, surprisingly, one of the cast-iron oval grenades she had so recently discovered near the site of the wreck. In fact there was a box full of them, laid neatly in a row, close to the hull, from which the sand had obviously been cleared quite recently.

Putting her finds carefully into the waterproof bag she had tied round her waist, Stella swam quickly after Kit to the cove where they had left the dive-ship anchored. To her surprise there was no sign of the ship's keel and she wondered if it had been moved to another part of the cove for some reason, but when she surfaced and looked about her all she could see was the smooth shimmering surface of sunlit water. The ship had gone.

Kit surfaced beside her and looked about him too, then pushing up his mask and removing his mouthpiece he said, 'Let's go ashore.'

'But where's the ship?' she asked having pushed her mask up too and got rid of her mouthpiece.

'Gone back to the resort, I guess,' he replied casually and turning over began to swim towards the rim of sand backed by the usual small palms and sea-grapes that curved about the cove. She swam after him.

'But the ship shouldn't have left without waiting for us to surface. It should have stood by. Surely Gerry and Matt know that,' she complained when, after she had reached the shore, Kit came forward to lift the harness holding her tank from her shoulders.

'Sure they know that, but probably Harriet was so mad when she found out I was diving with you that she insisted on being taken back to the resort to tell the professor that we'd eloped together,' he drawled with a touch of mockery. His hands lingered caressingly on her shoulders. 'I wish we had eloped,' he whispered and she felt his lips brush the nape of her neck.

A delicious shiver tingled down her spine and she turned to him quickly but he had turned from her and was laying down her diving gear on the sand next to his.

'What do you think of the wreck we've just looked at?' he asked in his casual way as if he hadn't touched her or said anything about eloping.

She unlatched her weight belt and let it drop to the ground, then removed her buoyancy compensator letting the air out of it.

'It's very interesting,' she said. 'But it isn't the *Santiago*. It's too small to have been a galleon.'

'That's my opinion too. I think it's the *Pelican* but I have no proof. I wish we could find some artefacts that are unmistakably English in origin and made in the right period, say late seventeenth or early eighteenth century.'

'I found some coins today,' she said, holding up her waterproof bag. 'Want to see them?'

'Sure. But let's get out of the sun and into some shade. We'll both get sunstroke if we stay out here.'

He led the way to a group of sea-grape trees and they sat down on the clean sand under the shade cast by the pale twisted trunks and thick, oval, green leaves. Two small lizards disturbed by their approach ran away, soon becoming a part of the patterns of the shadows.

'I think the coins are silver,' Stella said, taking her find out of the bag. 'I also picked up this.' She held up the broken piece of clay jar. 'And this.' She held up the grenade. 'There was a box of them that had been found recently. And Gerry and I found several of them in the crevasse, looking as if they had fallen there but I am quite sure they weren't in the crevasse yesterday or the day before that.'

He took the grenade from her turning it in his hand. 'The *Pelican* wouldn't have carried boxes of grenades,' he murmured. 'These are Spanish.'

'The box could have been part of the loot taken from the *Santiago*. In the records of the cargo and weapons carried by the galleon there is a reference to so many boxes of *granadas*.' She picked up one of the coins and began to rub it with the ball of her thumb. 'About the chest you pointed out. Did you notice it is padlocked?'

'I noticed that yesterday and I looked closely at the padlock. It was made in the USA. You know what I'm thinking, don't you?'

'You're thinking that the loot from the *Santiago* is in it,' she said slowly. 'You're thinking that Larry Lundgren found the treasure and hid it in that box.'

'That's right. And every time Harriet is in need of money she goes to the box, takes something of value from it and sells it. At least she gets someone to dive for it. And the way things are set up in these islands regarding the wrecks of ships that are within the offshore limit, there has to be a good reason for anyone diving and exploring a wreck. If there is any possibility of treasure being found on a wreck the government must know about it and take its share. So the story was cooked up about the *Santiago* wreck without treasure being found in the crevasse under the freighter so that an accredited diving company and an archaeologist with an international reputatiaon could put on a small expedition.'

'Then you don't believe that the *Santiago* wreck is in the crevasse?' said Stella, turning to him quickly.

'Do you believe those old timbers you've been

scraping at belonged to a Spanish galleon?' he
countered, his lips curling derisively.

She looked away from him at the shining sea,
her shoulders slumping as she realised that what
he had just told her only fitted in with her own
puzzled thoughts about the remains under the
wreck of the freighter after spending two and a
half days there searching and finding nothing.

'No, I don't,' she admitted with a sigh. 'And I
don't understand why Brian persists in searching
there . . .' She broke off as a sudden alarming
thought flashed through her mind. Turning to him
again urgently she said in a whisper, 'You don't
suppose that Brian went down yesterday afternoon
while we were absent to get something out of the box
for Harriet and at the same time removed some
grenades into the area where we've been diving to
provide something for Gerry and me to find, do you?'

'You're catching on, honey,' he drawled, the
Southern lilt very noticeable. 'He moved some
grenades there . . . to provide something that could
only have come off a Spanish galleon.' He paused
then added reflectively, 'Harriet was a bit too
obvious in suggesting that you go with me into the
village yesterday afternoon, I thought.'

'But Brian wasn't. He wanted me to stay with
him,' she argued.

'So why didn't you?' he challenged, giving her a
direct but mocking glance.

'You know why. I've told you why. I . . . I
wanted to be with you without anyone watching,'
she whispered.

Under the shade of green leaves and slender
grey twisted trunks the hot atmosphere suddenly
twanged with all kinds of sensual messages.
Having stated her position and revealed her

feelings to him, Stella waited for his response aware in every tingling nerve of his nearness and longing, as she had longed the previous afternoon, to touch him—yet afraid to, afraid that she might sink lower in his opinion than she had already.

'What are you going to do about the box in the wreck?' she asked, looking down at the coin in her hand rather than at him. Some of the tarnish had come off the coin. There was a dull gleam of silver and she could make out some letters. She continued to rub it with the ball of her thumb.

'Nothing,' he replied and lay back on the sand, supporting the back of his head on clasped hands. 'Right now, I'm going to take it easy on this beach since Harriet has made off with the ship and all the diving gear.'

'But if you're right, if the *Santiago*'s treasure is in that box, what are you going to do about it? Are you going to tell the government of the islands about it?' she demanded more urgently.

She wasn't going to look at him. She wasn't going to be betrayed again by her own desire to caress his sun-bronzed skin, to kiss his parted lips and be transported into a world of sensual delight. She wasn't going to give in to passion at noontime.

'I might mention it to Jack when he comes,' drawled Kit. 'Harriet hired him, not me, remember. And who knows? He could be in with them in the conspiracy to keep quiet about the treasure. He could have a share in it too, and I wouldn't want to be the person to betray him to any government authority. He would lose everything he's got if it was known he'd been a party to undersea piracy.' He turned his head, opened one eye and added enquiringly, 'What about you? What are you going to do?'

'I'll have to tell Brian,' she said. 'I'll have to tell him what I . . . what we suspect.' She looked down at the coin again. More tarnish had come off. She peered at it closely wishing she had the means to clean it properly. She scraped at the tarnish with a fingernail and found some figures. The letters that had appeared now formed a name.

'Kit,' she said excitedly, leaning over him. 'It's English. The coin is English and there's a date on it. 1701 and the name William. That would be William III. Do you know in which year the *Pelican* was lost?'

'September 1702, in a hurricane that lashed the islands and sank many ships.' He rolled over on to his stomach and took the coin from her. 'How many of these did you find?'

'Only two. But there might be more buried in the sand. I found this piece of pottery too. It looks like part of a Spanish clay jar, the sort used for carrying wine. Do you think such a thing would be taken as loot?'

'If it had wine in it, yes,' he said. 'But these only prove that the wreck on the other side was carrying some Spanish goods and was probably English. They don't prove that it was the *Pelican*. We'd need to see the treasure in that box to do that. We'd need to check it against the cargo lists in the records Brian has, to make sure it came from the *Santiago*.'

'Didn't you find any artefacts near that wreck?' she asked.

'Yes, I did.' He sat up and took something from the pocket of his swimming trunks. Lifting her left hand from her knee he slipped something over it and pushed it over her wrist and up her arm. It was a tarnished bracelet, two broad bands of silver joined together. 'I thought it might look good on you with a little cleaning up,' he said. 'I found this also.' He held up a gold ring between thumb and finger and then slid it on to the third finger of her left hand. 'It's a wedding ring,' he said softly.

The blood burned suddenly in her cheeks. With her head bent so that he couldn't see her face, she pushed the bracelet up her arm, admiring the elegance of it. The ring on her finger was a heavy and unfamiliar weight.

'They must have been among the loot,' Kit went on. 'And they must have come from a ship on which women were travelling. There were no women on the *Pelican*. They are the only bits of treasure I've found. I'd like you to have them, Stella. In remembrance.'

'Remembrance of what?' She looked up in surprise and found him very close, one sun-tanned knee pressing into her bare thigh, flames of desire blazing blue in his eyes.

'Our finding each other again. Our being cast up on a deserted tropical beach for an hour or two,' he murmured.

His hand cupped her chin and she watched his face with its wickedly slanting eyebrows, its cleancut piratical features coming closer. It was inevitable that this should happen once they found themselves alone again, she thought, feeling her own desire unfurl and leap up. Inevitable. No use either of them thinking they could stay aloof from each other for long. Even though it was noon and the sun was high in the sky they had to kiss and touch each other, they had to lie down on the shaded sand side by side, legs entwining intimately, hands seeking and finding sensitive pleasure-giving nerves.

'This is cheating,' she whispered teasingly as he shifted her under him.

'For you, perhaps, but not for me,' he replied with a touch of bitterness. 'I've just given you a ring. I noticed you don't wear the professor's.'

'Oh, Kit, what am I going to do? I thought if I told him about my affair with you he would back out, not want to marry me. But he didn't. I told him because I didn't want to cheat on him.'

'You could do the backing out. You could jilt him,' he pointed out, sliding a strap of her swimsuit down her arm, baring one up-tilted, rose-tipped breast.

'But I'm not sure . . .' She broke off with a gasp of pleasurable pain as his fingers pinched the soft smooth swell of flesh and skin. Involuntarily, her body arched against him, her lips parted, her head swam with all sorts of exquisite sensations.

'Not sure of what?' he asked, raising his head from her breast where his lips had been plundering.

'Not sure of you,' she groaned, still struggling to resist the waves of sensuousness that were beginning to flow through her, feeling that there was something contemptuous in his behaviour, a dark current of violence flowing beneath the subtle caresses with which he was arousing her. 'No, Kit. Please don't make me cheat,' she whispered desperately.

For answer his lips covered hers bruisingly. His kiss was like none she had known before not even from him. It brutalised her mouth and her cry of protest was lost in the heat of his mouth. And then suddenly everything changed as passion exploded between them and violence was transformed into a desperate aching need. No longer protesting, Stella responded instinctively to that need because she felt it too. Sensuousness swamped her mind. She lost all control and together they were swept along to a wild climax that left them both silent and panting, their bodies lax, all tension gone.

And in that sun-shot, noon-hot silence Kit withdrew from her and walked away.

CHAPTER SEVEN

SOMETHING touched Stella's leg; something that nudged her gently yet imperatively, urging her to wake up out of the delicious lethargy induced by sexual satisfaction. She opened her eyes and looked up, saw a long, bare, bronzed leg covered with gold-glistening hairs. Higher up, seemingly remote, a pair of blue eyes glinted down at her. She pushed herself to a sitting position.

'I must have fallen asleep,' she said, sweeping her hair back and realising at once that she was naked. As if in answer to an unspoken query as to the whereabouts of her swimsuit, the blue and white striped garment dropped from above on to her legs.

'Better put it on,' ordered Kit coolly. 'The dive-ship has come back and Gerry is coming ashore for us in the Zodiac. I'll go down to meet him and put the gear into the dinghy,' he added. 'Join us when you're ready.'

Still sitting in a strangely stunned state of mind, she watched him go from the shade of the trees and out into the blinding afternoon sun, his shadow marching beside him on the sand. Then she looked down at herself, at her bare skin so smooth, so delicately ivory tinted.

Had it really happened? Had she really submitted to his love-making? Or had she dreamed the exquisite pain and delight, the stolen delight they had shared in the culmination of passion, stolen because they were not entitled to it: she because she had promised to marry Brian, Kit, because ... Her thoughts stumbled and she searched for a reason as to why Kit had not been entitled to the pleasure they had experienced and found only the same one. He was not entitled to make love to her, to titillate her and coax her to soar with him to the heights of passion, because she had promised to marry Brian.

Hearing Gerry's voice so near as he talked to Kit while beaching the Zodiac, she stood up hurriedly, backed further into the shadows swimsuit in hand, and felt something slide down her arm. It was the bracelet Kit had placed there and on her finger was the ring he had given her in remembrance, he had said, remembrance of their meeting again and of being cast up on a deserted beach for a few hours.

Quickly she pulled on her swimsuit. Oh, it hadn't been a dream. He and she had really come together there under the dappling shadows of the sea-grapes. But it had been a dream spiced with bitterness, Kit's bitterness. There had been nothing gentle in his embraces or kisses. He had taken her in contempt at her behaviour and his own. She had felt his contempt in every move he had made and most of all in the way he had walked off and left her when the deed had been done. He had treated her as the cheat he still believed her to be.

And which she was, which she was, she groaned to herself. She had promised to marry one man yet she had made love with another because she loved him. She loved Kit not Brian. But she still wasn't sure of Kit's feelings for herself. She never had been sure even when she had lived with him. He was an enigma to her, a man who walked alone, who cared nothing for emotional commitment to a

woman, who had mocked her not so long ago
when he had slid the wedding ring he had found
on to her third finger.

Giving another flick to her hair, hoping she
didn't appear to be confused or emotionally
disturbed in any way, she walked out of the trees
and over the burning-hot sand to the dinghy into
which Kit was loading their diving tanks and
harnesses.

'Well, fancy you and Matt deserting us like
that,' she rebuked Gerry.

He made a face at her, pushing back fronds of
blond hair from his brow.

'If you'd heard that bitch carrying on, you
would have done what she wanted, too,' he
retorted. 'We were only allowed to come back for
both of you because the professor insisted.' Gerry
glanced sideways at Kit, put a hand beside his
mouth and whispered at her, 'The professor
seemed to think you'd been kidnapped by our
skipper. Couldn't get it into his head that Harriet
had made us desert you to bring her back. Are you
ready to leave your tropical paradise now and
return to face the wrath of your affianced
husband?'

In a way Gerry's humour was bracing, thought
Stella, as she stepped into the dinghy. It brought
everything into perspective. Of course she would
have to face Brian's anger when she returned if he
felt she and Kit had deliberately arranged things
so that they could be alone together. But his anger
would enable her to confront him with the truth,
with the fact that she knew about the secret cache
of treasure in a wreck which he had told her didn't
exist, in a place which he had said he explored with
Larry Lundgren and where they had found

nothing. Oh, yes, there was going to be quite a reckoning between herself and Brian when she got back to the resort.

'Did you show those grenades we found to Professor Haines?' she asked Gerry once they were on board the dive-ship and it was under way with Kit at the helm.

'I did. He seemed pleased but not excited,' said Gerry. 'You know I'm sure there was nothing like that near the cavity I was working on yesterday. I'm sure I would have seen them before this afternoon.' He looked at her, frowning in a puzzled way. 'If I didn't believe the professor is honest I would say he planted them there for me to find.'

'Planted them?' exclaimed Stella, feeling a cold uneasiness creeping through her. Supposing Gerry, who wasn't dumb by any means, guessed he had been tricked. Would he be as magnaminous as Kit and decide not to inform on Brian and Harriet to any authorities who might be interested? 'Why would he do that?'

'To keep us quiet. To make us believe we really are on the track of the wreck of the *Santiago*. I've been thinking for the past couple of days that those timbers in the crevasse are too light for any Spanish galleon. A few years ago, I helped salvage treasure from two galleons that were wrecked in the bay of Samana, in the Dominican Republic, around the years 1700 and, believe you me, their timbers were massive even though they had been drowned for a few hundred years.'

'But those are really Spanish hand grenades and the *Santiago* was carrying such weapons,' she argued, wondering first why she was protecting Brian, then realising that it was his reputation as

an archaeologist that was at risk and with his so
was hers because her name was linked with his,
not only professionally but also personally. She
wasn't only his assistant she was engaged to him.
'If they were planted, as you suggest, where did
they come from?' she asked Gerry warily.

'I haven't got as far as answering that question
yet,' he said. 'But I will.' He gave her a mocking
glance. 'I thought you would know,' he remarked.

She didn't answer him and was glad they were
approaching the jetty and that he had to jump
ashore with the ship's bowline. As soon as the ship
had docked she was off it and hurrying along the
jetty. She went straight to her room to shower and
change into a shift-like dress of coarse white
cotton that had a design of fishes painted on it.
While she was showering she noticed the bracelet
and ring Kit had given to her. She was going to
take them off when an idea occurred suddenly to
her. Tarnished though they were she would wear
them in front of Brian and see whether he
questioned her about them. Determined to make
the most of her appearance, she tied her hair at the
back of her neck, making it smooth and tight, then
hung dangling gold earrings in her ears. The style
made her look a little older and more sophisticated
than usual and with the white dress gave her an
elegance she didn't usually aim for. With high
heeled sandals on her feet she left the room and
walked through the plantation, up the steps of the
terrace and into the lounge. It was empty.

Hearing noises coming from the kitchen she
pushed open the swing door and looked in.
Virginia, the cook, was baking, singing some
calypso, as she worked, in a deep sonorous voice.

'Looking for Harriet?' she asked Stella.

'Yes.'

'She's in her room with the professor.'

'Which room? Her office, you mean?'

'No, her private sitting-room. Go through the door on the right of the bar. You'll come to it.'

The door to the right of the bar opened to reveal a short flight of stairs. Stella went up them to the top and entered a pleasant, airy room, furnished comfortably with wall-to-wall-carpeting, scattered armchairs and sofas. Through two sliding patio doors she could see a balcony. Reclining on a comfortable lounger was Brian. Opposite him, in a cushioned wrought-iron chair sat Harriet. Between them was a round, glass-topped table on which there were two tall glasses, one empty, the other half full.

Stella approached the open patio doorway, her footsteps silenced by the thick carpet. Neither Brian nor Harriet noticed her. Harriet was leaning forward and was talking in a low but insistent voice.

'What are you going to do about Stella?' the woman said.

'What do you mean by "do" about her?' demanded Brian irritably.

'Now that you know what she's like, that she's nothing but a tramp . . .'

'A tramp?' Brian was obviously mystified by the word and did not know the American meaning of it.

'A woman who sleeps around, has affairs with men,' said Harriet impatiently. 'How did you get to be so old without knowing anything about the real world, Brian?'

'As far as I'm concerned a tramp is someone who goes about in shabby clothing living on what he or she can pick up out of someone else's dustbin or by begging; someone without a home, always on the move.' he retorted.

'You mean a hobo.'

'No, *you* mean a hobo. Anyway, Stella isn't what you said she is. She's had one affair . . .'

'One that she has admitted to,' Harriet interrupted fiercely.' What about any she hasn't told you about?'

'I don't want to know about any others,' Brian picked up the half-full glass and emptied it at a gulp.

'No, of course you don't,' said Harriet sweetly. 'No man likes to hear that he's been taken for a ride by a woman, made to believe she is innocent and wholesome and, oh, so fresh.'

Deciding she had heard enough of this conversation which had made her ears burn, Stella stepped back into the room then advancing more noisily she tapped on the glass of the patio door.

'So this is where you two are hiding,' she called through the mesh screen that covered the opening. 'Mind if I join you?'

'No, of course not. Come right through, Stella,' said Harriet at her brightest and breeziest. 'Here, take my chair, I was just going down to mix another drink for Brian. Can I get you one?'

'Please. One of your Planter's Punches would be fine,' said Stella. 'No, don't get up, Brian. How is your ankle? Is the swelling up or down?

'It's up and really painful,' said Harriet before Brian could speak. 'I'm so sorry, Stella, that I was forced to leave you this morning. Those two pirates had weighed anchor and were steering out of the cove before I knew what they were at. Nothing I said would make them turn back. They were under orders from Barlow, apparently, to bring me back here. I'd like to know why. Do you know why?'

Only just able to prevent herself from gasping at what seemed to be a bare-faced lie on Harriet's part, then wondering suddenly whether it was the crew of the dive-ship, Kit, Gerry and Matt, who had been lying and had arranged between themselves that Harriet should be removed from the scene of the diving operations while Kit and herself were underwater, Stella could only stare at the woman in stupefied silence.

'Harriet thinks Barlow arranged the whole thing so that he could get you to himself for a few hours,' said Brian quietly. 'Did he, Stella?'

She turned to look at him. Apart from the way he was frowning at her in his schoolmaster fashion, as if she were some miscreant he had to punish, he looked very well, quite sun-tanned in fact. He looked as if he had been cosseted and waited upon and she guessed he had—by Harriet.

'No. At least, I don't think so. Gerry told me that Harriet insisted that he and Matt bring her back here when she found out that Kit had dived with me against her orders,' she said coolly, looking him straight in the eyes. His own eyes flickered, the eyelids drooped. She was glad he had the grace to look discomfited by what she said. But Harriet wasn't. Harriet had gone, was crossing the room inside on silent feet, avoiding confrontation. 'Either Gerry or Harriet is lying, Brian. I wonder which one?' she added smoothly.

He shifted on the lounger, shaded his eyes with one hand and looked out at the view, looked anywhere in fact but at her.

'Brian, I have something to tell you,' she began

softly. 'A confession to make. Another one. I went over the reef, to the bay on the other side. I went with Kit and he showed me the wreck he had found under an outgrowth of coral. We went into the hull. There was a chest there, a cheap modern one, fastened with a padlock.'

She finished speaking and sat back. It was up to him now, either to lie to her or tell the truth. He glanced quickly at her, then stared, his attention caught by the bracelet on her left arm and then drawn to the finger of her left hand on which the wedding ring hung.

'Where did you get that ring?' he demanded hoarsely, sitting up straight.

'This? Oh, Kit gave it to me. And this.' she turned the bracelet on her arm. 'I'm going to clean it as soon as I can. I suspect both are Spanish, part of the loot taken from some galleon, perhaps by a privateer whose ship was wrecked on the other side of the reef. Kit found them near the wreck in the sand. Where is the rest of the loot, Brian? Is it in the padlocked box?'

'So you've seen it.' He sank back against the cushions, his face pale. 'Barlow found it, of course,' he went on bitterly. 'I told Harriet I didn't like her leaving you alone with him.' He opened his eyes and gave her a reproachful glance. 'What is he going to do about it? What are you going to do?'

'Kit says he isn't going to do anything except tell Jack Cowan when he comes and leave him to deal with it.'

There was no doubting that Brian was relieved. Relief showed in the sudden relaxation of his body, in the clearing of his face.

'And you? What about you?'

'I . . . I think I'd be satisfied with an explanation from you,' she murmured, leaning forward in her chair. 'Brian, is it the loot from the *Santiago* which is in there? The jewels, the silver and gold?'

'I have only Larry's word for it. He said he had found the *Pelican* with the treasure in it. He collected it all, or at least as much as he could find on several dives he made by himself. He was going to bring it up and declare it to the island government but Harriet wouldn't let him. She said she needed it. She needed the money that the sale of some of the jewellery would bring to pay her debts on this place. She had some sort of hold on him and threatened him that he'd regret it if he didn't put it in a box and leave it in the wreck locked up, and whenever she wanted any of it he was to go down and fetch some of it up for her. Poor Larry. He hated doing it. He longed to show the treasure to prove that he had found it, have the artefacts cleaned and dated and put in some museum. Then he died and Harriet had no one she could trust to go down and fetch something else for her to sell. So she made up the story that the *Santiago* had been wrecked on the reef, invited me to be in charge of the search, got Jack Cowan to agree to provide the dive-ship and equipment as he always had for Larry, and then applied for and received permission to put on this little exploratory expedition of ours.' He sighed and ran his fingers through his hair so that it stood up in all directions. 'I had no idea what it was she wanted me to do until we arrived here.'

'You should have told me at once,' she said softly. 'You should have shared the secret with me.'

'Maybe I should,' he agreed. 'As it was it was

difficult for me to get to the wreck of the *Pelican* and open up the box with you and Gerry always diving with me and Barlow looking on. Harriet got impatient so she sent you and Kit off to the telephone, commandeered the ship, and I went down yesterday to open the box and take some jewellery out for her.' Interest and his usual lively curiosity in all things of historical significance livened his sallow face for a few moments. 'You should have seen it, the treasure, I mean. Beautiful pieces, of gold decorated with diamonds and emeralds, exquisite glassware, some of it of German and Bohemian origin proving, as we've always guessed, that the laws limiting Spanish ships to Spanish-made cargo were ignored and contraband often exceeded the legitimate cargo. There were coins too. Doubloons.' He gave her a wary glance. 'There's my explanation for what it's worth. Now I have to ask you if you're going to go to the representative of the government on this island and tell him about the box and what is in it.'

She sat silent for a while, turning the tarnished wedding ring round on her finger, battling with her conscience. A droning sound in the sky drew her attention. A small plane was approaching. She watched it swoop down over the main building of the resort guessing it would land on the airstrip on the other side of the road.

'The charter plane from St Thomas,' murmured Brian. 'I hadn't realised Harriet was expecting more guests. The season is practically over. She's planning to leave for the States at the end of the month.'

'And take the piece of loot with her, I suppose,' remarked Stella drily. 'If I did go to the authorities with a story about the box what would she do,

Brian?'

'She would tell the world that we had been in a conspiracy with her late husband to hide the treasure.' His thin lips tightened into a bitter line. 'And that would be true of me if not of you, because I agreed to do what she asked. She says she would blacken all our reputations, mine, yours, Jack Cowan's, Kit Barlow's, Gerry's, Matt's, say we had conspired to defraud the island government as well as her.'

'But would anyone believe her?'

'I'm afraid they would. She has the government superintendent for this island in the palm of his hand. The business she brings to the island in the way of tourists, sports fishermen and, probably in the future, divers, is very necessary to the economy. Without the few resorts like this one there would be no work for the local people. Oh, yes, Harriet would be believed and we would appear as desperate pirates, out for what we could get in the way of treasure and no better than Nathaniel Barlow who looted the *Santiago* and scuttled her.'

'Kit is really a descendant of Nathaniel,' Stella said. 'He told me that the story of the loss of the *Pelican* soon after the *Santiago* had been looted is among the records of his family. If it could be proved that the wreck on the other side of the reef is the *Pelican*, could he and his brother lay claim to the treasure?'

'I don't really know. I wouldn't think so. Nathaniel stole those valuables. They really belong to the Spaniards who were on the galleon or were waiting for them to be delivered. Now they belong to whoever finds them and the government of the islands.'

They were both silent for a while. Stella thought of Kit saying he would tell Jack Cowan about the box in the wreck and leave Jack to deal with it. What would Jack do? Supposing he wasn't a party to Harriet's scheme to keep the treasure for herself? Would he go to the government and blurt out the truth, risk all their professional reputations?

'So what are you going to do, Stella?' Brian asked.

'Nothing,' she replied, as Kit had done to her, and smiled. 'At least, not yet. I'll wait until Jack Cowan comes and see how he reacts. If he was with Larry Lundgren when he found the treasure he could be in the conspiracy with Harriet, couldn't he? And that would account for her disappointment when Kit came with the ship instead of Jack.'

'Yes, I suppose that's a possibility,' said Brian. Again he looked very relieved. 'I'm glad you're not going to do anything hasty, Stella. Do you forgive me for getting you involved? If I'd known what Harriet had in mind I would never have asked you to come and assist me.'

And if Brian hadn't asked me to come with him I wouldn't have met Kit again and be sitting here feeling terribly guilty for having cheated Brian this afternoon, she thought.

'I forgive you,' she said slowly, looking down at the ring on her finger again, turning it round and round. She would never part with it, she thought. Even though Kit had been in a bitter humour when he had slipped it on her finger, she would keep it all her life. In remembrance of him and the love she had always felt for him. Oh, if only Kit loved her as she loved him, she would tell Brian now that she didn't want to marry him. Perhaps she should tell him now. She studied him from under her lashes. Why had she agreed to marry him? Why? Because in England at the university working with him all the time, she had come to believe that she was fond of him. But it was not only that. She had seen an advantage to herself in marriage to him. As his wife she would be able to insist that she accompany him on all his archaeological expeditions. As his wife, she could make a name for herself as an archaeologist. Fame had been the spur, she thought wryly, that had prodded her into agreeing to marry him.

But why had he proposed to her? What had she to offer him? Very little. Only her intelligence, her ability in recognising and dating artefacts, her skill at diving taught her by Kit. What else did she have? No fortune, certainly. A well-shaped body, a fairly attractive face. She shuddered suddenly at the thought of being made love to by Brian and glanced at him again. Was that why he had asked her? Somehow she didn't think so.

'Barlow had no right to give you that bracelet and ring,' Brian spoke suddenly startling her, and she sat up straight dropping her hands on her lap. 'It is part of the treasure and should be declared. Give them to me.'

'No.' She leaned back as far as she could in her chair away from him as if she suspected he might reach out, seize the jewellery and drag it off her.

'Why not?' he demanded. There was a vicious curl to his thin-lipped mouth now and his eyes glared at her.

'Because I want to keep them,' she retorted, glaring back at him.

'Because he gave them to you, I suppose,' he

said with a sneer. 'Because he was once your lover.'

'Yes, because he was once my lover,' she repeated, facing him with dignity, glad it was out now, in the open.

'I don't understand. I don't understand how you could . . . could do what you did, live with him on his yacht, sail about with him, be his . . . his . . .' he paused, swallowed then forced the word out, 'his mistress. It . . . it just doesn't fit in with my conception of you. I feel as if I've been really deceived by you in more ways than one.'

'Then you won't want to marry me,' she looked at him steadily. 'Now you've found out that I'm not the sort of woman you thought I was.'

'Stella, if only I could believe that you don't . . . I mean, that you and Barlow haven't——' he began in a stumbling way, his face contorted by the discomfort he was feeling in having to be frank with her.

'If only you could be certain I'm not in love with him any more. Isn't that what you're trying to say?'

'I suppose I am. You went off with him yesterday afternoon . . .'

'Only at Harriet's contrivance,' she put in quickly.

'And then today you've been alone with him for several hours during which time he gave you those,' he gestured towards the bracelet and ring.

'And so you can't help being suspicious,' she accused him. 'Well, that's enough for me. I don't want to marry a man who is going to be suspicious of me all the time. I think we'd better retract from that promise we made to each other before we left England, Brian. Perhaps we were too hasty in making a commitment. Perhaps some time apart from each other would be good for us. After all we have been working closely together for the last three years . . .'

Her voice trailed off into silence as she realised Harriet had come back and was standing where she had stood earlier, behind the screen door to the patio. Behind Harriet loomed another figure, short and wide-shouldered.

'Hello, Harriet,' said Stella smoothly, rising to her feet. 'You can have your chair back . . .'

'Oh, don't worry about that.' Harriet slid back the screen door. Her square-jawed face was smiling and there seemed to be nothing false about the smile for once. She was really in a good humour, brimming over with cheerfulness. 'Jack has come at last,' she announced, stepping out on to the balcony. 'Come on, Jack. Don't be shy. Come and be introduced. This is Jack Cowan, Stella. Brian, you remember Jack, don't you, from when you were here two years ago diving with Larry.'

The short wide-shouldered man dressed casually in jeans and T-shirt came on to the balcony. He had black curly hair and his skin was very swarthy. A black moustache curved above his mouth and black hairs matted his forearms.

'Pleased to meet you, Stella,' he said quietly. 'Nice to see you again, Professor Haines,' he added politely, going over to shake Brian's hand. 'I hear you've had a little accident that's put paid to your diving for a while.'

'Jack just flew in from St Thomas,' said Harriet turning to Stella. Now there was something triumphant in her smile. 'Kit will be leaving on the same plane.'

'When?'

'Right now,' said Jack. 'At least, as soon as the pilot is ready to take off.'

'Oh, it's great to have you here, Jack,' said Harriet gaily. 'It hasn't been the same without you. Has Kit told you anything about the diving?'

'He told me that he found the box,' said Jack calmly, leaning back against the railing of the balcony. 'I should have known he would go exploring on his own. You can't keep a good diver like Kit on board a dive-ship when it's anchored at a good place to dive. I'm sorry, Harriet. It's my fault he found it.'

'What is he going to do?' exclaimed Harriet. All her gaiety had faded rapidly. Her face looked drawn and anxious.

'Nothing. He's not going to say anything about it to anyone. I explained the situation to him, and he asked me to assure you he would keep mum because he has realised he would risk damaging his own reputation as a diver as well as mine, and also the reputations of Professor Haines and his assistant, as you had pointed out to him, if he did spill the beans to the government.'

'Thank God for that,' said Harriet weakly, and collapsed on to the chair Stella had vacated. 'If you knew how worried I've been. I should have followed my instincts. I should have sent him packing as soon as he arrived. I guessed he spelled trouble with a big T. Why the hell did you send him, Jack?'

'Because I knew you were desperate to have someone dive. And because I trusted him. He's one great guy, Harriet, as he's proved by not betraying us. He's one of the best friends I've ever had and he hasn't let me down.' He looked across at Stella who was hovering by the open screen door. 'What we don't know is how far we can trust Miss Grayson, now that she knows about the box.'

'Stella has said she will do nothing,' said Brian. 'We have just discussed the matter.'

'Oh, good,' sighed Harriet. 'Thanks, Stella.'

'You're welcome,' said Stella coolly. 'But I think you should declare the treasure to the government, Harriet. You'll feel much better if you do. And there could be things in there, important historical artefacts that should be cleaned and examined, dated and catalogued, and shown to the world. Since it is known that Brian has been searching here for artefacts from the *Santiago* it wouldn't seem strange if he brought some up, a few at a time . . .'

'But the government would take half of the treasure,' protested Harriet. 'And I want it all.'

'Stella has a good point, though, Harriet,' interposed Brian. 'Some of the stuff in there you could never sell without rousing suspicions. I think we should consider her suggestion seriously. I'm quite willing to do what she suggests, bring up some of the most historically significant pieces and report my finds to the government. I'd feel a lot easier in my conscience too. What do you think, Jack?'

'Sounds great to me.' He looked across at Stella again and this time he smiled at her. 'You're a pretty smart woman, Stella. That plane should be about ready to take off now.'

It took a second for his remark to register. Then she realised suddenly he was conveying a message to her. Kit would be leaving soon, within seconds.

'Excuse me,' she muttered. 'There's something I have to do.'

Finding her high heels impeded her progress down the stairs she took them off when she reached the lounge and ran out to the front of the main building in her bare feet. Tiny stones on the rough surface of the road pricked her soles as she crossed it, but she could hear the roar of the plane's engine and couldn't slow down. Running as fast as she could she went through the clearing in the bushes and trees that edged the air strip and straight towards the white and blue six-seater monoplane that was at the end of the runway. Kit was at the doorway of the plane handing up a bag to someone inside.

'Wait, wait,' Stella shouted breathlessly, but he didn't look round and she realised he couldn't hear her. With a final burst of speed she flung herself forward and reached the plane just as Kit was climbing aboard.

'Wait, oh Kit, wait,' she gasped and stretching up touched his leg.

He looked around, saw her and dropped down to the ground.

'I have something to tell you before you leave,' she whispered, her chest heaving.

'Really?' Hands on his hips in typical stance he looked down at her with ice-blue eyes. 'What?'

'I think we . . . that is Brian, and Jack and I might be able to persuade Harriet to let Brian bring up some of the stuff in the treasure box and declare it as important historical artefacts,' she panted. 'Brian didn't know what she wanted him to do until we arrived here. He wouldn't have gone along with the idea if she hadn't blackmailed him by saying she would besmirch all our reputations if he declared the stuff to the government. I thought you'd like to know that I think she'll be relieved if that is done.'

'Thanks for coming to tell me,' he said coldly. 'Is that all you have to say? If so, I'll be getting aboard.'

'But wait,' she put a hand on his arm. 'Won't I ever see you again?'

She looked up at him pleadingly, her heart in her eyes although she didn't know it. He looked down at her, his face still set in hard lines, his eyes frosty.

'That's up to you, Stella,' he drawled. 'You have to make a choice. You know now I've no time for women who cheat. You can't have Haines and me. I'm sure he feels the same way. So long?'

He heaved himself up into the plane. The door was shut. The plane taxied along the runway, gathering speed, and took off, wobbling a little but gaining height, and circled above her before going straight as an arrow towards the westering sun, seeming to split the blue arch of the sky.

Feeling more disconsolate than she had ever felt before in her life, Stella made her way back slowly across the road and up the path to the main building of the resort. As she stepped into the lounge and picked up her tossed-aside shoes, the door to the right of the bar swung open and Jack Cowan came into the room.

'Did you catch Kit?' he asked, his small black eyes twinkling with interest.

'Only just,' she said. 'Thanks for the hint.' She sat down on a sofa and began to slip her sandals on. She was still feeling winded and shaky after her high-speed run.

'You were with him, weren't you, a few years ago? In St Thomas?' He sat down beside her.

'How do you know I was? I don't think you and I have ever met before,' she said in some surprise.

'Kit told me. When he came to see me a week or
so ago. I was telling him about this job I'd been
commissioned by Harriet to do and I told him the
names of the archaeologists. He recognised yours
straight away. It was then he offered to come in
my place. I guess he wanted to see you again.
Must have given you a shock when you met him
again and weren't expecting to,' he said with a
chuckle. 'Kit always was one for surprises.
Mischief is his middle name.'

'Yes, I was surprised,' she admitted. 'I suppose
he's gone back to his yacht. He said he had a new
one and had cruised down to St Thomas. Will he
be sailing back to Nassau, do you know?'

'Guess so. Leaving tomorrow, he said.'

'Which way will he be going?'

'Said he'd make straight for San Juan. Puerto
Rico. If the weather co-operates he'll do it in a day
and a night. Then over to Puerto Plata, in the
Dominican Republic, another long overnight run.
Might take him two whole days. He's going to
visit friends there. After that straight through the
Bahamas and up to Nassau. I wouldn't think he'll
make many stops in the Family Islands but will
press right on, sailing day and night,' said Jack
casually.

'Alone?' asked Stella.

'I dunno.' Jack shrugged his heavy shoulders.
'He might pick up a crew in St Thomas. A lot of
the guys who crew on the charter yachts like to
leave and go back to the States this time of the
year and they're looking for free rides.' He rose to
his feet. 'Well, I'll get back to the ship. Seems like
we've persuaded Harriet to do what you suggested.
And I must say it's a great load off my mind. I
didn't feel too happy about her hiding that loot

even though she offered some of it to me as bribe
to buy my silence. I'll be seeing you later when the
guys and I come up for dinner. And then there'll
be the pleasure of diving with you to bring up
some of that treasure.'

He left her with a wave of her hand and she
walked over to the door beside the bar, went up
the stairs. Harriet and Brian were still on the
balcony and Harriet was still talking. She stopped
when Stella slid open the screen door.

'Jack says you've agreed to let us bring up some
of the treasure,' Stella said.

'Yes.' Harriet sighed. 'He and Brian have
convinced me it's the most sensible thing to do.'
She sighed again then gave Stella an under-browed
glance. 'I guess you think I'm a real swindler,
hanging on to that stuff, taking it piece by piece
and hawking it round fences I know in the States
trying to get a good price for it.'

'I certainly think it hasn't been very honest of
you,' said Stella rather stiffly.

'Mm. I thought you might,' said Harriet drily.
'But, then, you don't know what it's like to be up
to your ears in debt and to have all that stuff just a
dive away from you. It was a temptation I couldn't
resist. Have you ever been tempted and not able to
resist, Stella?'

There was a double meaning in the question that
Stella wasn't blind to. Harriet was implying that
she had faced temptation recently in the form of
Kit and had not been able to resist.

'I suppose I have,' she murmured.

'Anyway,' Harriet swept on. 'I'm hoping that
what you think of me won't stop you from
continuing to dive to help bring up the artefacts.
Brian insists that you have to do it while he's

incapacitated. He says you will know what to
bring up. You'll recognise the pieces of historical
significance that Jack and the others won't.'

'You will, won't you, Stella?' said Brian.

She glanced at him. He knew she couldn't refuse
because she was his paid assistant. Only if she
resigned her position here and now could she
refuse. And there was still the matter of whether
they were going to be married or not to clear up.
Meanwhile, Kit was going further and further
away from her.

'Please, Stella,' said Harriet softly, standing up
and putting an arm around her waist. 'It is your
idea. And it's what you came out here to do, to
discover the treasure of *Santiago*. Just think of
what a feather in your cap it will be when you
come up with some of those artefacts.'

Stella looked from Harriet's bland and shining
face to Brian's taut, lined one. She had a choice to
make. She could say no. It's up to you, Stella. You
have to make a choice. It's either Haines or me.
Kit's parting remarks mocked her. It looked very
much at the moment as if it was going to be Brian,
she thought miserably. Better the bird in the hand
than two in the bush, she mocked herself.

And then suddenly some strange spirit of
independence rose up within her. Why should she
do as Brian asked? Why shouldn't she please
herself and leave, go after Kit and show him that
she wasn't committed any more—that she was as
free as air, free to go with him if he wanted her?

'No,' she said, coolly. 'I'm not going to do it. As
soon as it can be arranged I'm leaving Sanada and
going to St Thomas.' She glanced at Harriet,
surprising an expression of mixed surprise and
triumph on the woman's face, that was immedi-

ately changed to one of regret. 'Perhaps you can tell me how I can do that?' she added.

'Be glad to,' replied Harriet.

'But you can't go. I forbid you to go,' Brian shouted and both Stella and Harriet turned to him. He had swung both legs off the lounger and was glaring at Stella.

'Forbid me?' she exclaimed angrily, all her sense of feminism aroused by such blatant male arrogance. 'Neither you nor any other person has the right to forbid me.'

'I do. I'm head of the department in which you work and I'm also going to marry you,' he retorted.

'No, you're not. Not any more. I'm resigning from my position in the department right now. I'll let you have it in writing as soon as I can put pen to paper.'

'But what about your doctorate?' he spluttered, staring at her as if she been transformed into some stranger from outer space.

'To hell with that!' she exploded, taking an example from Kit's way of speaking. 'And I'm certainly not going to marry a man who thinks he can forbid me from what I want to do. As someone recently pointed out to me, marriage between you and me would be most unsuitable.'

'It was me,' said Harriet with a little crow of triumphant laughter. 'I pointed it out to Stella. I pointed it out to you too, Brian, dear. But don't feel too badly about it. You need someone to look after you, who'll be around cooking a meal for you when you come home or down from cloud nine wherever you scholars spend your time. Someone like me.'

'I don't understand, Stella,' Brian bleated. 'You can't do this to me.'

'That's the problem. You never have understood me. We belong to different generations between which the gap is very wide,' she explained, her anger fading and sympathy for him taking its place. 'The only bridge across that gap has been our mutual interest in history and archaeology. And that isn't enough. I realise that now. And I think you do, too, in your heart.'

'But I love you, Stella,' he argued.

'No. I don't think you do and I don't love you. We admire and respect each other's intellectual ability, that's all. We would both be very unhappy if we were to marry. As Harriet says you need someone to provide your meals on time when you've finished studying and thinking, someone who will listen and not argue with you; someone to relax with and be comfortable with.'

He stared at her for a few seconds and then raised his shoulders in a slow shrug. 'Perhaps you're right,' he admitted. 'But I wish you'd stay and do that diving, bring up those artefacts.'

'No. It's better that I leave, make a clean break. Gerry is pretty good. He's worked on searching wrecks of Spanish ships. All you have to do is tell him what to look for and what to bring up.'

'But there's all the arranging and dating to do, the cataloguing,' he complained.

'Well, you'll just have to do that yourself, won't you?' she replied lightly. 'You'll have the time while you're resting your ankle, won't he, Harriet?'

'Sure he will,' said Harriet. 'But you won't be able to get away until tomorrow. The mail-boat comes in then from Roadtown. You can go back there on it, and from there you can catch another ferry to St Thomas. I'll drive you in to the village in the morning.'

CHAPTER EIGHT

As she had promised, Harriet drove Stella in the truck to the village of Portland next day to catch the ferry-cum-mail-boat that visited Sanada twice a week. The weather was as usual sunny and warm and windless. In the wide bay the water glowed with its usual emerald and turquoise colours and above, the sky was a bright sunny blue and, as yet, cloudless.

'I guess you're hoping to catch up with him,' Harriet said, unable to stay silent for long, wanting to know what was going on.

'With whom?' asked Stella coolly.

'Oh, you know whom I mean,' snorted Harriet. 'You and Brian, you're so damned particular about the way you speak. Makes us ordinary folk feel put down. Kit Barlow, I mean. He's in St Thomas. Left his yacht there. I suppose you're going to join him on it?'

'I don't know. I haven't made any plans,' replied Stella. 'I have to go to St Thomas, as you know, to get to anywhere else.'

'I still can't get over you breaking off with Brian,' Harriet burbled on. 'Of course, I think you did the right thing. And you needn't worry about him. I'll look after him. Why, I should think by the end of the month he'll have got over it and be thanking his lucky stars you did break it off.'

Harriet changed gear noisily and swung the truck away from the bay, past the small group of native houses, where the usual gardeners waved a greeting and she and Stella waved back.

'I was asking Jack about Kit last night,' Harriet went on. 'He was a mine of information. Seems Kit is really well heeled since his father died. Neither he nor his brother have to work, although they both put in an appearance now and again at the shipping company's offices. That's why Kit is able to sail about the islands and offer his assistance as a diver on a voluntary basis, helping at various wreck sites or ocean research underwater labs. He was over in England not so long ago diving at a wreck site there. Guess he didn't look you up, then?'

'No, he didn't look me up,' murmured Stella suppressing a pang of pain because he hadn't even tried to find her.

'There's a lot of women after him—you know the sort, looking for a rich guy to marry and then divorce him for a huge settlement. You'll have a hard time catching him.'

'I'm not expecting to catch him,' said Stella wearily. 'Oh, I wish you'd stop going on about him. I know he isn't interested in marriage. Neither am I at the moment.'

'He was going to marry, though, one of the women off the charter boat told me. She thought the woman was Sherri Golden, the Golden Mines heiress. I wonder what happened? I guess it fell through. Either she changed her mind or he changed his. Jack didn't know. Kit's never said anything to you about it, I guess?'

'No, he's never said anything to me about it,' said Stella thinking of Sherri, blonde and leggy with a clear, carrying voice. 'Harriet, about the treasure,' she went on, determined to change the course of conversation, 'it might be a good idea to inform the superintendent of this island that something has been found as soon as you can.'

'Oh, I am. As soon as I've dropped you off I'm going to visit Amos Saunders,' replied Harriet. 'It's a pity you can't stay to meet him and his wife, Hazel. She's the most gorgeous woman. Has that coffee-coloured skin, you know? And her figure, *wow!*'

Harriet went on to gossip blithely about the local government representative and to answer Stella's questions about how the islands were ruled and the rest of the drive to the village passed by without any further reference to Kit Barlow.

At the wharf, the ferry-boat had already docked and was filling up with passengers, mostly islanders who were going to Roadtown to shop and winter residents who were returning to the States, Canada and even Britain after six months in their tropical hideaways. Harriet dropped Stella off, said goodbye casually and drove away without a backward look. In the saloon of the small but sturdy boat Stella sat between two large black women and as the boat ploughed across the thirty-five-mile stretch of water that separated Sanada from the next island in the group, she had plenty of time to think about all that had happened since she had first arrived on Sanada.

Only five days had gone by yet it seemed like a lifetime during which she had run the gamut of emotions as her love for Kit had revived, rising like a flame from the ashes of a desire which she had believed to be dead. And now she was on her own again, unattached, strictly single. Now she knew that Kit had been guilty of cheating too. When he had been engaged to marry a woman called Sherri he had been living with her, making love to her. He had been cheating on Sherri as much as she had cheated on Brian yesterday. Oh,

God, was it only yesterday that passion had flared up between them at high noon?

Two of a kind, she supposed they were, she and Kit, both liking to be independent, both reluctant to make a commitment, both believing in free thinking and free love. Yet drawn magnetically to one another and unable to resist the passion of physical attraction.

No wonder Brian, conventional and a little timid emotionally, couldn't understand her affair with Kit. How cool Brian had been this morning when she had said goodbye to him. But, then, Kit had been in an Arctic mood too when she had parted from him yesterday. Both men had made her feel as if she were the one who was at fault, a typically masculine reaction to a woman who was able to act independently of them.

She looked out at the tranquil blue water. The other islands were appearing now, mountainous and covered with sparse green vegetation, rimmed with yellow sand, floating in emerald-green shallows. The boat twisted through a narrow passage between some dangerous rocks then surged out into the broad expanse of blue water named after Sir Francis Drake. For a while Stella daydreamed, imagining what it had been like for those early adventurers and explorers when they had first come across the Atlantic and had seen what must have seemed like paradise to them.

Across the strait to the entrance of a wide bay the ferry plunged. They passed anchored freighters, moored yachts and marinas spiky with masts on the approach to the Roadtown ferry wharf. Soon Stella was aboard another ferry, leaving the harbour fast, and travelling further down the channel between other high islands on her way to

Charlotte Amalie, St Thomas, capital town of the
US Virgin Islands.

The harbour at Charlotte Amalie was, as usual,
crowded with yachts at anchor among which the
ferry had to nose its way to the wharf. Buildings
glittered, flags fluttered and traffic was heavy
along the road that curved beside the bay. For a
while, bewildered by so much noise and business
after the quiet seclusion of Sanada, Stella stood
outside the building where she had cleared
customs and immigration and which was close to
the ferry dock, not sure what she should do next.
She had left without any real plan. To get away
from Brian and Harriet was all she had wanted to
do, to act independently as if in control of her own
destiny.

'Taxi, ma'am.' An elderly black man approached
her.

'Yes. Yes, please,' she murmured, and he raised
a hand to wave to one of a fleet of taxis waiting in
a car park near the customs building. One drove
forward, her bags were put into the back seat with
her, the door was slammed and the driver turned
in his seat to ask her where she wanted to go.
After an initial hesitation she said,

'Yacht Haven marina.'

After all it was the only place she knew in St
Thomas, the place where she and Kit had docked
Siren four years ago and the place where Jack had
told her Kit had left his new yacht *Dolphin* while
he had been in Sanada. She knew also that there
was a hotel near the marina where she could stay.
She was on holiday, she reminded herself, as the
taxi swept out into the road and joined the traffic
going east. She had two whole weeks left before
she could fly to England from Miami on her

return ticket and also before her money ran out, she added ruefully to herself.

The taxi dropped her off in a courtyard that she remembered from her last visit, planted with palm trees and colourful blossoming shrubs. Many people were coming and going up a flight of shallow steps. Picking up her bags Stella went up them, turning right into the foyer of the hotel. After registering she was shown to a room overlooking the marina where numerous boats gleamed in the sunshine, tied up to the wooden docks.

Taking her time she showered, changed her clothes and went down to the restaurant for a sandwich and a cold drink. She was, she discovered, having great difficulty in restraining herself from getting up and rushing down to the marina office to ask the whereabouts of a yacht called *Dolphin* and its skipper. But it wouldn't do to approach Kit in that way. She didn't want him to think she was pursuing him. She just wanted him to know she had made a choice and that she hadn't chosen Brian Haines. Once he knew, the next move would be up to him and it was quite possible her choice would make no difference to him.

When she had eaten she strolled slowly down to the group of buildings where the dive-shop and the marina office were situated. For a few moments she lingered by the dive-shop peering in through the windows past the diving gear, swimsuits and other nautical clothing that were on show, to the counter inside, trying to make out whether the same people worked in the store. She recognised neither of the two young women.

She was just turning away from the store when

she collided with someone who was passing behind, her, a dark-bearded, dark-haired hulk of a man, Bob Dawson.

'Well,' he drawled, his dark brown eyes dancing with mockery. 'What are you doing here?'

'I'm on my way back to Britain, really,' she said coolly. 'Stopping over before catching a plane to Miami.' She remembered their last meeting and added rather awkwardly, 'Bob, I'm sorry about the other evening at the Pelican's Roost. I did recognise you and remember you, but I . . .'

'It's OK. Kit filled me in,' he replied, his eyes losing their warm merriment and becoming harder as their glance swept over her. 'Your professor here too?' He jerked his head towards the hotel building.

'No. I'm here alone. I was thinking of having a look at the yachts.' She paused, waiting.

'If you were hoping to find Kit, you're too late,' he said in a cold flat voice. 'He left early this morning.'

Disappointment surged through her. Not until that moment had she realised how much she had been hoping to find Kit.

'Do you know where he was bound for?' she asked hurriedly. Bob had half turned away from her as if eager to be on his way. He glanced down at her with hostile eyes.

'Why should I tell you?' he retorted nastily. 'You're going to be hitched to the professor so why go chasing after Kit? Like me he doesn't care for two-timing bitches.'

She tried not to flinch at the insult. Stiffening a little she tilted her chin at him and said calmly,

'I'm not chasing after Kit. I had thought that if he was here I could give him a message, an answer to a challenge he made before he left Sanada.' She managed a careless shrug. 'But as he isn't here, I can't do it, can I? And since you're so interested,' she went on with a touch of sarcasm, 'I might as well tell you I'm not going to be hitched to the professor. He and I have split. Nice seeing you, Bob.' She turned away from him to walk along to the marina office.

'He's headed for San Juan,' Bob called after her. 'Should be there by tomorrow. After that Puerto Plata.'

He didn't follow her, nor did she go into the marina office. There was no need. She knew now that Kit had left. She turned off along one of the docks, pretending she was admiring the various yachts that were tied up, stern first, but hardly seeing them because her mind was leaping ahead, wondering how she could get to San Juan tomorrow. Suddenly she was no longer taking her time. Whirling round she almost ran back along the dock, past the office and the dive-shop and up the ramp to the hotel. At the telephone she thumbed hastily through the directory searching for a travel agency. Soon she was talking to a travel agent who in a few minutes had her booked on the morning flight to San Juan. Leaving the hotel Stella caught a taxi and drove into Charlotte Amalie to pick up and pay for her ticket and also to get the travel agent to book her a room in a hotel in San Juan. That done she spent the rest of the afternoon wandering around the pretty arcades and passages of the town visiting boutiques and well-known stores buying gifts for her sister, Audrey, and her children.

She slept badly that night as she wondered whether she was doing the right thing by going to San Juan, always ending the argument with herself

by saying she was merely island-hopping for her
own pleasure to use up the rest of her spring
vacation, and if she happened to run into Kit at
any of the places she visited, well, she ran into
him. Not for anything would she admit to herself
that she was going to the places he might be in
because she wanted desperately to see him again to
put everything right between them, because even if
nothing came of another meeting with him, she
had to part friends with him.

The flight to San Juan the next day was
uneventful above a glittering blue sea dotted with
green islands. Heavy purple clouds wreathed the
mountains of Puerto Rico and the landing was
made in a fierce shower of rain. A taxi shared with
an American businessman whisked her to a high-
rise hotel on Condado Beach, and after lunch she
walked to the nearby Club Nautico at the eastern
end of the San Juan canal, and then on to San
Juan marina on the other side of the canal. The
Dolphin was docked at neither.

Assuming that Kit hadn't arrived in port yet,
she returned to the hotel and spent the afternoon
on the beach swimming a little and sunbathing.
Later, when it was somewhat cooler and the
western sky was streaked with feathery gold-lit
clouds and flushed with crimson light, she walked
again to the club and the marina, to be told that
no boat had arrived that day from St Thomas.

She spent the evening at the hotel not wanting
to risk going into the centre of town alone at
night. In spite of the comfort of her surroundings,
the exotic foods, she felt lonely and not a little
depressed, thinking about Kit and wondering
whether he was still at sea or whether he was
groping his way into the harbour.

Next morning she was at the two docking areas early but could not find him or his boat. It was suggested to her that the best way of finding out whether he had entered San Juan harbour would be to go to the US customs where he would have had to report on arriving, so she went by taxi to the old town to the 'most beautiful custom house in the Americas', an imposing, pink building close to the ferry landing. There were several yachts tied up near the landing but not one of them was the *Dolphin*. Kit hadn't reported to customs and none of the skippers on the visiting yachts clearing customs had seen him or his yacht nor had they heard him on their radios.

'Where would he be bound after San Juan?' asked one of the skippers, a grey-haired man with a weatherbeaten kindly face who had been cruising the Caribbean with his wife in their ancient ketch and were now on they way back to Florida and home.

'Puerto Plata.'

'Could be he's gone on there without calling here. Weather is pretty good out there right now. We would have stayed out only we needed to pick up some supplies and make a few phone calls. Of course, there's always the possibility he's put in at Samana on his way to Puerto Plata.'

Thanking him for his suggestions, Stella wandered away along the narrow cobbled streets of the old city which had once been enclosed by the walls of Fort El Morro and Fort San Cristobal. Decorative wrought-iron balconies hung above her and elegantly shaped gas lamps jutted from walls. Windows were covered by iron grilles set into massive heatproof walls. She walked right out to Fort El Morro to climb the wall running

along the edge of the headland guarding the
entrance to the harbour. Waves pounded at the
foot of the cliff and beyond them the sea,
turquoise blue under the hot sun, stretched away
to the dark line of the horizon. Wishing she had
binoculars Stella looked out, searching the wide
waste of water for a sail and saw none.

Two hundred and eighty miles from San Juan to
Puerto Plata by sea, so her acquaintance at the
ferry landing had informed her. At a reasonable
speed that would take a yacht like *Dolphin* about
forty-eight hours. If Kit had sailed on instead of
coming into San Juan, reckoning from the time he
should have arrived at the port yesterday
afternoon, he would arrive at Puerto Plata, barring
mishaps, some time tomorrow afternoon or
evening. Unless he put in at Samana.

Oh, why was she bothering? Why didn't she just
stay here a few days then catch a plane to Miami,
change the time of her flight to Britain and go
home? Why hang about the islands hoping to see
him in some port?

Because she didn't want to go home. She wanted
to linger among the scented tropical islands where
life was so unhurried and, above all, she wanted to
find Kit again and tell him she had made her
choice.

Going back to the old town she searched among
the shops and found a travel agency. Yes, she
could fly to the Dominican Republic, to Puerto
Plata airport. When would she like to go? After a
great deal of discussion with herself, Stella decided
to stay another whole day and two nights in San
Juan, just in case Kit arrived there and made a
reservation to fly the day after the next.

Arrangements for her departure made, she

proceeded to try to enjoy her stay in Puerto Rico. After lunching at one of the better-known restaurants in the old city she returned to the hotel for *siesta*, then some swimming and sunbathing. In the evening she walked down to the marina and Club Nautico to check on the yachts without result. The *Dolphin* was still not there.

Determined not to hang about the next day as if waiting for Kit to arrive she booked to go on a tour of the countryside arranged by the hotel. The bus drove into the mountains along winding paved roads through the lush vines, giant tree ferns and flowering trees of the rain forest, and past vast coffee plantations. There were flocks of vivid coloured parrots and parakeets, and the air was soft and warm. The day passed pleasantly for Stella in the company of two other single women who were on holiday from the States. When she returned to San Juan she checked again that the *Dolphin* was not at either of the marinas, and had dinner with her new acquaintances at a downtown night-spot.

Next morning she visited the customs building again to make sure the *Dolphin* had not arrived in San Juan then drove out to catch the plane to Puerto Plata. A few hours later she was in a taxi driving to the old silver port. Since it was the week before Easter Sunday, it was Festival time and the narrow streets and wide plaza, with its elegant two-towered Spanish church, blazing flowerbeds and shady pathways, were packed with people, mostly teenagers. Noise blared from radios advertising the wares of shops. Small motorcycles, more than Stella had ever seen anywhere, dodged between cars and buses, ridden not only by swarthy-skinned, T-shirted men but also by similarly dressed young women.

With the help of a Spanish phrasebook Stella
had asked the taxi driver to take her straight to the
harbour, and from the *plaza* the cab slid down a
steep street lined with shabby shops. The street
ended in an open area obviously created by the
demolition of some buildings. The ground was
rough and pitted with potholes. Dark warehouses
loomed beside the dirty heaving water of a
harbour where several yachts were anchored.
Other yachts were tied up at a wharf near by. On
the opposite side of the harbour, against another
wharf, a big cruise ship gleamed with white paint,
flags fluttering from it in the stiff breeze. And
towering over it all, behind the scattered buildings
of the city, soared the distinctive shape of the
mountain Isabella de Torres, steep-sided and
covered with thick vegetation.

She paid off the taxi when it stopped at a
gateway in a fence protecting the nearest wharf,
using the *pesos* she had bought at the airport. The
cab went away and she was alone with her two
bags. The hot sun shone down on her bare head
and sweat prickled her skin. Opening the phrasebook she searched for words and made up a
sentence. Then picking up her bags she walked
towards the gate and the hut beside it.

In the hut was a dark-faced security man. She
answered his query in Spanish in her own
stumbling version of the language, asking him if he
could tell her whether or not there was a yacht
called *Dolphin* either anchored in the harbour or
tied up at the wharf. When he shook his head
negatively and said he didn't understand she asked
him if he spoke any English. His answer was
negative. She tried Spanish again with a similar
result and was beginning to feel desperate when a

small truck drew up beside the fence, parking a little beyond the security man's hut where other vehicles were parked.

A young woman with shoulder-length blonde hair got out of the truck, slammed its door shut and strode towards the gateway. She was dressed in a pretty cotton skirt and a white sleeveless blouse. As she approached the security guard she smiled and greeted him in Spanish. He smiled back, at once losing all his dourness, then said something quickly in Spanish gesturing to Stella. Immediately the young woman swung towards Stella, her grey eyes sparkling in the shadow of the white sun hat she was wearing perched on her head.

'Oh. He says you're English,' she said. 'So am I. Can I help you? Joe says he thinks you're asking about a yacht. My name is Liz. Liz Benitez.' She held out her right hand.

Stella introduced herself and asked again if Liz knew if there was a yacht called *Dolphin* at the wharf or in the harbour.

'It's not at the wharf. I'd know if it was because that's our boat there, that huge black schooner, and most of the people who tie up at the wharf come aboard to see us.' She laughed merrily, white teeth flashing. 'You see we're a sort of fixture here, Juan—he's my husband—and I. We sailed into this harbour having crossed the Atlantic three years ago and have been here ever since. We run a bar on board for visiting yachtsmen and Juan tries to help them all he can by finding supplies for them, or finding mechanics or riggers to repair their equipment. But why don't you come on board? Juan is sure to know if the yacht you're looking for is anchored out there.'

With a few short sentences in Spanish Liz explained to the security guard that she was taking Stella to her boat; he nodded and they passed through the gateway, leaving Stella's bags in his care. They walked along the wharf to the black schooner. Its stern was wide and slanted. Its name was *Chiquita* and there was a gangway leading on to its afterdeck from the wharf. Stella followed Liz on to the boat and waited on deck while Liz went below to find Juan. Above, the two raked masts festooned with rigging glinted gold against the brilliant blue of the sky. Beneath her feet the wooden deck swayed slightly as the yacht was rocked by the fierce surge that slopped against the wharf.

It wasn't long before Liz appeared again followed by a slim, black-haired, olive-skinned man whom she introduced as her husband. He was dressed immaculately in white cotton trousers and a white shirt and his sleek hair looked as if it had been polished. His lean face was creased by laughter lines, his brown eyes snapped and sparkled with good humour and his wide white grin was welcoming as he shook Stella's hand.

'So you are the one,' he said somewhat enigmatically, then added as if in an aside to Liz, 'she is a friend of Kit's.'

'Are you?' Liz looked most surprised. 'Oh, why didn't you say so? I know Kit is here, on his boat out there in the harbour. I just didn't recognise the name of the boat. Shall I call him, Juan? On the radio. Tell him to come ashore.'

'*Si, si.*' Juan's face creased even more into lines of impudent humour. 'But do not tell him why he is to come. Make a big mystery out of it. Or better still, tell him the port commandant wants him at

once. There is something wrong with his papers
and if he doesn't come ashore now he will be
arrested.'

Liz nodded, mischief also glinting in her face
and went down below.

'The customs people here are very strict,' Juan
went on to explain. 'They come aboard your yacht
when you enter and when you leave you must go
when they say so and they see you off the premises
very often.'

'When did Kit arrive?' asked Stella. Now that
she knew he wasn't far away she was beginning to
wish she hadn't come. What would he say when he
came ashore and saw her here talking to Liz and
Juan?

'Yesterday afternoon. He sail all the way from
St Thomas,' said Juan.

'He isn't answering,' said Liz, appearing in the
companionway that led into the pilot-house of the
schooner. 'Are you sure he is on board?'

'Sure I am sure,' answered Juan. 'Did I not see
him rowing out there in his dinghy only half an
hour ago? I called to him but he did not answer
me. Hand me the binoculars.'

Liz ducked back into the pilot-house and
reappeared with the glasses. Juan took them and,
striding up to the bow of the schooner from where
he could get an uninterrupted view of the
anchorage, looked out. Hardly had he looked than
he let out a yell and came hurrying back to them.

'*Por Dios*, he is pulling up his anchor.'

'He can't be leaving already,' said Liz. 'He only
arrived yesterday. And he wouldn't leave without
saying goodbye, surely.'

'Who is to know what Kit will do?' said Juan.
'Come,' he said to Stella, 'come with me. I will

take you out to him in my dinghy. When he sees you he won't leave.'

'Oh. No. It doesn't matter. I only wanted to tell him something. It isn't really very important,' stammered Stella.

'Of course it is important,' said Juan looking fierce. 'If you have come all this way to see him it must be important. Come on.'

Taking hold of her hand he pulled her with him towards the gangway.

'Please, Senor Benitez, Juan,' she gasped. 'It doesn't matter . . .'

'You are the one who was with him a few years ago, in St Thomas, hmm?' he asked, turning on her so abruptly she was forced to stop.

'Yes. But how do you know?'

'That is where I first met Kit. We had just come, Liz and I, and our crew, across the Atlantic from Spain.'

'But I didn't meet you. I don't remember seeing you there.'

'We were anchored offshore, in the harbour. I met Kit at the customs office. He said he had a woman crew. And then last night when he came ashore for a drink he told me had met you again on a diving expedition in Sanada. But we waste time explaining. He will have that anchor up and be gone before we are in the dinghy. Come. This way.'

A Zodiac was tied up with other dinghies at the end of the wharf and they climbed down an iron ladder set into the wall to reach it. Stella was glad that she was wearing trousers. Soon they were zooming across the greyish brown water where all sorts of debris floated. The outboard engine roared, yachts were passed, spray flew. Looking

ahead, Stella saw a silvery grey yacht growing
bigger and bigger as they approached it. From the
stern of it water spouted indicating that its engine
was going. On its foredeck a man in shorts but no
shirt was pulling in on the anchor line. His bronze
curls blowing in the strong breeze were haloed
with sunshine. Then the Zodiac was swerving
under the stern of the yacht and turning to nudge
against the port side.

'Up with you,' ordered Juan. 'Go on, jump
aboard.'

'But——' began Stella. The dinghy was bouncing
up and down on the waves and so was the yacht. It
was going to be tricky getting aboard. Timing
would be everything.

'Go on, quickly,' roared Juan, who was
obviously used to getting his own way.

She stood up, put her hands on the rail of the
yacht and heaved herself up until she was able to
stand on the rail. Then she swung one leg over the
life lines and then the other and stood on the deck.
She looked down at the dinghy but it had gone,
was rushing round to the bow of the yacht.
Holding on to mast shrouds she hurried forward.
Kit had stopped hauling on seeing Juan in the
dinghy and was yelling something to the Spaniard
who yelled something back. Juan waved his hand,
and the Zodiac zoomed off away from the yacht.
Stella rushed over to the other side.

'Juan, come back. Come back,' she yelled, but
he only grinned and zoomed on.

'What the hell are you doing here?' said Kit
behind her, and it seemed to her that every word
he spoke clinked with ice.

She turned to him slowly. He was standing in
typical pose, hands on hips. He was bare footed

and bare chested. His eyebrows slanted in an angry frown and his eyes, ice blue, appraised her through half-closed lids.

'I have something to tell you. I . . . I wouldn't have come out here only Juan made me come.' She glanced over her shoulder to the speeding dinghy but it was out of sight although she could hear the roar of its engine.

'Well, now you're here, you can help,' said Kit coldly and authoritatively. 'Go aft and put the engine in forward gear. I'll have to motor up to the anchor to break it out.'

'But I haven't come to help. Oh, please re-anchor and take me ashore in your dinghy.'

'No. I've cleared customs and the officials are on the wharf there watching and making damned sure I leave.'

'Surely you could explain to them that you had to put me ashore before you could leave,' she argued, pushing her hair from her face.

'What do you have to tell me?' he asked abruptly.

'Just that I've made a choice and I felt you had to know.'

He was very still. Only his eyes moved as they searched her face.

'So?' he queried.

She caught her hair with both hands pressing it down against her head so that it wouldn't stream across her face. The deck heaved under their feet, the engine throbbed, the wind whined in the rigging, and waves slopped against the smooth hull of the yacht. She licked her lips and drew a deep breath.

'I'm not going to marry Brian Haines,' she whispered. 'Now, will you please re-anchor and take me ashore?'

'No.'

He spun on a heel and went back to the cockpit,
pushed a lever beside the wheel and the tune of the
engine changed. Leaping from the cockpit he went
forward again, avoiding her by going along the
port-side deck and began to haul on the anchor
rope as the boat moved gently forward. When the
chain appeared he ran aft, took the engine out of
gear, went forward again and pulled up the rest of
the chain. The anchor clanked as it came up
against the steel roller on the bow.

'You can't do this,' Stella shouted against the
noise of the engine, the wind and the water. 'You
can't take me away against my will. It's nothing
short of kidnapping. I won't go with you. I won't.'

He didn't answer, but after making sure the
anchor was fixed in place and the rope and chain
had disappeared down the hawse pipe into the
chain locker below he hurried back to the cockpit,
pushed the gear lever, increased the speed of the
engine and began to steer the boat out of the
anchorage towards the buoyed entrance.

'I won't go with you. I won't,' Stella raged as
she stepped down into the cockpit and glared at
him, standing in front of him, the wheel between
them.

'My dear, you have no choice,' he retorted,
smooth as silk, but she thought his grin was
wolfish and apprehension tingled along her nerves.
'Unless,' he went on, 'you want to swim for it in
that filth.'

She glanced over the side at the dirty, tea-
coloured water and could scarcely suppress a
shudder at the thought of swimming in it. Yet
beyond the filth, beyond the shabby docks, there
was beauty; the soaring green mountains, em-

purpled where clouds hovered over their summits in rolls of silvery grey vapour; the droop of palm fronds over flashes of pale sand; the natural beauty of the island of Hispaniola, considered by Columbus when he first saw it to be the most beautiful of all the islands in the West Indies.

'I was going to go on the funicular railway to the top of Isabela de Torres, tomorrow. I was going to buy amber in the market,' she grumbled. 'Kit, please go over to the wharf, put me ashore.'

'No.'

'But I left my bags by the gate. I have no clothes with me.'

'I'll call Juan on the radio. He'll get your bags and send them on.'

'To where? Where are you going?'

'To Nassau. Here, take the wheel and steer while I go and call Juan now before we're out of range.'

And so she found herself behind the wheel, steering a strange boat out of harbour between red and green buoys which marked a channel between a wicked-looking reef of rocks and a spur of land on which the remains of an old fort stood.'

When Kit returned to the cockpit he was wearing a white shirt and sunglasses.

'It's done,' he said crisply. 'Juan will send your bags by air to Nassau and they'll be waiting at the airport when you get there.' He glanced about him. 'You can change course now,' he said and gave her the numbers of the compass course she should follow. 'I'll hoist some sail.'

'But Kit,' she protested. She had also looked around and had seen, now that they were clear of the harbour, seemingly endless turquoise sea ridged with rolling waves. There was no land other than the island behind her in sight. 'Where are we going?'

'I've told you. Nassau.'

'But it's miles away from here. Won't we stop anywhere on the way?'

'No. I've delayed long enough on this trip,' he replied roughly. 'We'll keep on sailing day and night up through the Bahamian Family Islands. There's plenty of food on board and plenty of fuel for the engine if we have to motor. We'll be in Nassau in about a week with a bit of luck.'

'Supposing there's a storm?'

'We'll ride it out.'

She considered him for a few moments: the lean, tanned cheeks dented with humour lines, the long, curling lips, the tough, angled jaw, the strong column of neck. This was the man she loved, the only man she had ever loved, from whom she had parted once believing she would never see him again and whom she had found again only to earn his contempt and disrespect.

'Kit, I don't understand,' she complained. 'I don't understand why you're doing this. Why you won't put me ashore?'

He looked back at her and she felt irritated because she couldn't see the expression in his eyes hidden as they were by the sunglasses. One corner of his mouth curled downwards.

'Maybe I don't understand myself,' he drawled. 'Maybe I don't understand why you followed me just to tell me you're not going to marry Haines,' He leaned towards her, his lips widening into a sardonic grin, 'And maybe, just maybe, we'll both begin to understand by the time we get to Nassau. Now, let's concentrate on sailing for the next few days, shall we? We'll take watches like we used to do, four hours on and four hours off, and we'll share the cooking. At night we can use the autopilot or the wind-vane instead of steering and just keep watch on that. You know the drill, Stella, and it should be a good sail if this weather holds and I think it will. Put all personal problems aside and enjoy a few days of sailing.'

He stepped up on to the deck and went forward to the mast to start making preparations for hoisting the mainsail. Stella looked down at the black face and white numbers of the compass before her and swung the wheel a little to starboard to alter course. Put all personal problems aside and enjoy the next few days, he had suggested. But how could she when he was her personal problem and he was going to be close to her for those few days? His attitude towards her hadn't softened. Telling him that she wasn't going to marry Brian had done nothing for her; it hadn't been a magic wand which she had waved in the hope that Kit would be transformed immediately from a contemptuous lover into an adoring suitor who wanted to marry her.

How could she enjoy a few days of being alone with him knowing that they were going to part in Nassau? How could she go through the trauma of having to leave him again? There must be something she could do to win back his respect— to win his love.

CHAPTER NINE

FROM the bow of the *Dolphin* Stella looked down into the clear, blue-green water through which the yacht was sailing. The wind was on the beam filling the shiny white mainsail and billowing out the silvery green and grey striped cruising spinnaker. Overhead the sun was shining out of a clear blue sky across which little white puffs of cloud occasionally floated. It was the last day of their cruise through the Bahamian Family Islands and they were crossing the tail of the Yellow Bank, an area of shallow water lying between the Exumas and New Providence Island. She was on watch for the dark brownish loom of coral heads beneath the surface, the dangerous pinnacles which could rip through the hull of a boat, wrecking it, and which had to be avoided. Every so often she would stick out an arm to point either to right or left to indicate to Kit, who was steering, so that he could swing the wheel and the boat would miss danger by a few inches.

In about two hours they would be in Nassau harbour, nosing their way into the marina where Kit kept his boat. Memories of the last time they had come this way together and had parted so abruptly and coolly rushed in on Stella and she bit her lip wondering how she could avoid a repetition of what had happened three and a half years ago. Nothing during the last five days could lead her to the conclusion that it might be avoided. Kit had been coolly polite to her. There had been no intimacy between them at all. He hadn't touched her and she hadn't touched him although there had been times when she had ached to break down the barrier of pleasant but distant friendliness he had erected between them.

During those days and nights they had shared the sailing of the yacht between them they had worked easily together as a team. She had obeyed his orders as she always had, acknowledging that in the matter of sailing a yacht and navigating it through treacherous passages between the islands he was her superior. When he had spoken to her it had always been about the weather, the courses he wished her to steer, the performance of the yacht or to name the islands among which they sailed. A few times she had tried to direct the conversation into more personal channels but when she had, he had always moved away to another part of the boat or suggested she rested while she could when it had been his turn to be on watch.

A shout from him drew her attention and she looked back.

'We're over it. You don't have to look out any more,' he called.

She wandered back to the cockpit and sat down, aware as she had always been aware, of his physical presence, of the bronze sheen of his bare skin, the muscular symmetry of his arms and legs, his shoulders and chest. Physically he hadn't changed since the last time they had sailed together but she knew now after these last few days that he had changed as a person. No longer the light-hearted, irresponsible playboy she had known, he was harder, more serious. He had always been self-reliant and independent but now he was self-contained, refusing to share thoughts and ideas with her, as withdrawn and deep as some underwater cavern and somehow in the next hour before they reached Nassau she had to try and plumb those depths.

'I still don't understand,' she murmured, 'why you insisted on me coming with you to Nassau. It would have been so easy for you to put me ashore at Puerto Plata and I could have gone home from there.'

'Home?' he queried. 'Are you going back to England?'

'Yes.'

'To get that doctorate? Won't it be difficult studying under a professor after jilting him?' His voice was spiced with mockery.

'I'm not going back to that university,' she admitted. 'I'm going to resign from my position as an assistant lecturer. I . . . I'll find somewhere else to take a doctorate. I might even try an American university.'

'Why didn't you stay to help bring up the treasure?' he asked casually. Behind the wheel he sat relaxed, sun-hat tilted forward over his eyes to shade them from glare instead of the disguising sunglasses. She had told him what had happened on Sanada after he had left. He knew all about the convincing of Harriet to declare the treasure to the island's government.

This was it, she thought. This was her chance to plunge into the depths.

'After you had left I didn't want to stay,' she said quietly. 'You said I had a choice. I made that choice. Now I'm free again.'

'You didn't have to follow me to tell me you'd made it,' he pointed out drily.

'I know. But I . . . I wanted you to know.' Oh,

God, how difficult it was to break down her own pride and admit to him that his opinion of her was important. 'I didn't want you to go on thinking badly of me,' she added in a low voice. 'You called me a cheat. You made love to me as if ... as if I were a ... a ...' She cast around for some word that he would understand and remembered Harriet describing her to Brian. 'As if I were a tramp,' she finished, her voice shaking suddenly with anger at the memory of the way he had walked off and left her on the beach near the reef the day they had been deserted by the crew of the dive-ship.

He glanced at her sharply, blue eyes glinting brightly within the shadow of the hat brim.

'I made love to you because I couldn't help it even though it was against my own code of behaviour,' he retorted. 'I don't like to share a woman with another man,' he added, his voice grating. 'Any woman who wants me has to be mine entirely.' He paused, then said while she stared at him in surprised silence, 'If I seemed more violent than usual and possibly casual in my behaviour afterwards it was because I was angry with myself, angry because I could be so easily seduced by you from keeping to my own principle.' He gave her another under-brim glance, a slow, sultry glance which made her nerves quiver. 'You're the only woman who has been able to do that to me, Stella.'

'You ... you behaved as if you hated me,' she whispered.

'I did. But I hated myself more because I wasn't able to resist either you or my own desires. It was a difficult situation and one which I found myself regretting I'd landed myself in when I found out you were going to get hitched to Haines. It was my

own fault too. My own damn fool fault. I went to
Sanada because I knew you would be there. God
knows what I hoped for.' Again his voice grated
bitterly. 'Here, take the wheel. Looks like we're
running out of wind. I'll start the engine and check
that we're on the right course for Porgee Rock
light at the entrance to the harbour.'

He sprang down the companionway and Stella
took over the wheel. All around the water was
blue and limpid, rippled only slightly by small
waves. Ahead there were smudges of islands on the
horizon and the triangular sails of yachts
glimmered faintly in the heat haze which had built
up during the afternoon.

Was she any further along the way to resolving
her problem? A little. At least she knew now why
Kit had behaved the way he had. He had gone to
Sanada because he had known she would be there.
He had wanted to meet her again and had found
the situation bedevilled by her engagement to
Brian. What had he hoped for? To renew their
affair? Probably. And now that she knew how it
had been with him, didn't she regret that
everything had been fouled up by her own
behaviour to him when they had met again?

The engine throbbed into life. Kit reappeared
and went forward to drop the sails. The boat
surged forward. Islands grew bigger and more
distinct. She could make out the shapes of houses
and other buildings. By the time the mainsail was
furled, the sail cover in place, and the foresail
reefed in around the forestay they had reached the
harbour entrance. Kit went down to call harbour
control on the radio to ask permission for entry, as
was the rule at Nassau. He stayed down below for
a while making it impossible for her to continue a

conversation with him and she wondered ruefully
if he was doing it deliberately. He had met her
again, the situation had not been to his liking and
so he had left and she had been foolish enough to
follow him.

Within half an hour they were docking at the
same slip at which they had docked three and a
half years ago. The same dock master was there to
take their lines. The buildings of the harbour club
were just the same. The same palm trees clustered
in the courtyard about the swimming-pool. There
was even the same tall, leggy woman with long
blonde hair coming along the dock and calling out
to Kit in a clear, high voice. The only difference
was that the woman was pushing a buggy in which
a sun-hatted child sat.

Oh, it was too much to face, thought Stella
miserably, as she ducked down into the cabin so as
not to be seen by the woman who was now kissing
Kit affectionately. She couldn't go through it
again. She couldn't leave him and fly back to
England and spend weeks, months regretting
having left him. But what could she do?

In the cabin she hastily took off the pair of Kit's
shorts she had been wearing and pulled his over-
sized T-shirt off. She had just dressed in her own
white pants and sleeveless shirt when she heard
footsteps on the deck and the voice of the woman
called Sherri coming nearer. The woman was on
board.

There was no way of escape. She had to stay
there in the cabin, making a pretence of getting
everything ship-shape, putting away the charts
they had used in the drawer beneath the chart
table.

'Sherri, I'd like you to meet Stella Grayson who

has been crewing for me from Puerto Plata. Stella, meet Sherri Barlow, my brother Tom's wife.'

Stella turned slowly, hoping her amazement was not showing on her face and tried to smile at the blonde woman who was carrying the toddler in her arms and eyeing Kit's crew with a curiosity she didn't bother to hide.

'Hi, Stella. This is Nathaniel Barlow. Shake hands with the pretty lady, Nathaniel, and say "hello",' said Sherri.

The little boy put out a chubby and rather sticky hand to Stella and burbled something which could have been, 'Hello, pretty lady'. His soft skin had a golden sheen and his long-lashed eyes were a brilliant ice-blue.

'Hello, Nathaniel,' Stella said. 'Hello to you, too, Sherri. I didn't know Kit had a sister-in-law.'

'Oh, Tom and I have been married nearly three and a half years.' Sherri, who had greenish-grey eyes that twinkled with good humour, grinned suddenly and impudently. 'I was supposed to meet you once before but you left before we could get together. You might have come to my wedding if you'd stayed on, but there was something about a degree you wanted to get and which was more important to you. By the way, your luggage has arrived at the house. So, why don't you come along there now with me and Nathaniel in my car? I'm sure you're longing for a bath or a shower and a change of clothes. Kit will come along after us. His car is parked here.'

Stella turned to Kit. He was leaning against the chart table, hands in the pockets of his shorts and seemed to be completely unconcerned with the conversation.

'Will that be all right?' she asked. 'Should I go with Sherri?'

'Sure.' He shrugged. 'I'll see you later.'

She followed Sherri ashore and only once looked back at the *Dolphin* but Kit had stayed below. Supposing he didn't come along after them as Sherri had suggested he would? Supposing he decided to stay on board the yacht rather than come to a house where he knew she would be? What would she do then? Leave Nassau without saying goodbye to him? Without making another attempt to clear the air between them with more explanations?

The car was a handsome cream-coloured Cadillac. Stella sat in the front beside Sherri and Nathaniel sat in his car seat in the back. Sherri drove with a seemingly careless grace that Stella secretly envied, turning sharply left off the main road into Nassau, explaining that at that time of day the traffic would be impossible in the middle of the town and so she would go through the outskirts and then drop down on to the shore road to Lyford Cay.

'I did see you three and a half years ago when we docked at Nassau,' said Stella. 'But I thought then and I've since heard that you were engaged to marry Kit.'

'You did?' Sherri let out a little trill of laughter. 'Oh, that's priceless. Does Kit know?'

'No. I've never told him.'

'But you should. It'll give him the biggest laugh. What ever made you think he was going to marry me?'

'When you came down to the dock to greet him, you flung your arms around him and kissed him and said, "Now we can be married. Now we can set the date." Or something like that.'

'I meant, of course, now *Tom* and I can be

married. We—I mean Tom and I—had been waiting for Kit's return. Tom wanted him as best man at the wedding.' Sherri glanced sideways at Stella. 'But you said you'd since heard Kit and I were once engaged.'

'Yes, someone on Sanada, the island I've been visiting said she'd heard he was once engaged to marry Sherri Golden, the heiress, but it had fallen through.'

'Never. Not Kit and me. Tom and me. She must have got the brothers mixed up. Oh, it's all so crazy. Kit and me? Never in a hundred years. We're just not suited. And never yet have I met the woman who could get him to agree to the commitment of marriage. He's a real loner. Always has been.' Sherri stopped talking while she negotiated a difficult corner. Once they were on another road, going west past small houses set in gardens ablaze with bougainvillaea and hibiscus she added, 'I wish he would marry, though. So does Tom. We both feel he's getting restless again. But what about you, Stella? No commitments for you either?'

'I would like to get married,' Stella found herself saying much to her own surprise. 'I would like to have a child.'

'Well, maybe you and Kit ought to get together. After all, you have sailed together a lot and being together on a small yacht is a really good test for compatibility. I should know because I went cruising with Tom before we were married. We're off again on *Dolphin* in a day or two, going to take Nathaniel for about a week, see if he likes it. That's why Kit came back so we could have the boat. We put a deadline out for him to meet. He might never have come back if we hadn't.' Sherri sighed. 'He's really hard to tie down.' She slanted Stella another glance. 'But I guess you know that.'

'I know some things about him but not everything,' murmured Stella.

'Do you have to leave immediately, go home to England?' asked Sherri.

'No. I don't have to but I probably will ... unless something happens to stop me,' said Stella in a stifled voice.

'Then we'll just have to see that something does happen, won't we?' said Sherri gently. 'You're welcome to stay as long as you like at the house.'

Conversation became more general as the car took a downhill road to the right, then to the left again to curve beside the sea, past the big hotels on Cable Beach, and out on the road to the western point of the island. The hotels gave way to villas hidden among clustering trees and Stella recognised the road along which she had travelled with Shirley and Josh Masters over four years ago on her way to a party.

She recognised also the entrance to the driveway with its stone gateposts and the pink-washed, Spanish-style house with its rounded arches, wrought-iron balconies and purple creeper. And when she followed Sherri into the big room where the party had been held, her heart quailed and she felt a rush of terrible regret because there was no tall stranger there staring at her across the room with blazing blue eyes.

Instead there was another stranger, a shorter, darker man whose eyes were blue but did not have the brilliance of Kit's. He was Tom Barlow and he welcomed her pleasantly to the house.

'Kit's on his way,' explained Sherri. 'Stella's come for her luggage. She's going to stay here for

a few days.' Sherri turned to hand over Nathaniel
to his nanny who had just appeared, then swung
back to Tom. 'I must talk to you, darling. I have a
little plan to discuss with you. As soon as I've
shown Stella to her room.'

The room was big, on the second floor. It was
furnished with a king-sized bed covered in a blue
and green print. The walls were painted ivory
against which simple pine chests glowed. On one
wall there was a long wardrobe with sliding doors.
Opposite, arched windows opened on to a
balcony. Through a door to the right of the bed
Stella glimpsed a tiled bathroom. Her luggage had
been placed on a cushioned bench at the foot of
the bed.

She didn't unpack completely. Although Sherri
had told Tom she would be staying a few days she
couldn't be sure that she would. Only if something
happened to stop her from going back to Britain
would she stay. Only if Kit asked her to stay
would she stay.

In the exotic bathroom, exotic to her because it
had a whirlpool bath set into the floor and
numerous mirrors in which she could see her
reflection from all angles plus huge fluffy towels,
she wallowed in hot water for a while, shampooed
her hair and then soaked again. When she was dry,
she draped herself in a towel and decided to search
for a hair-drier. She found one in a cupboard
which was full of male toilet requisites; shaving
foam, razors, after-shave lotions. The previous
guest to stay in that room must have forgotten to
pack them when he had left.

Her hair dry she returned the drier to the
cupboard and padded over the pale blue carpet
into the bedroom to dress. As she slipped into the

other dress she had brought with her, a pale turquoise cotton printed with a darker blue pattern, a simple design with a V-neck, no sleeves and a tight fitting skirt slit at both sides, she had the strangest feeling that the room had a 'used' atmosphere, unlike most guestrooms she had stayed in. Although neat and spotless the bed looked as if it was often slept in. The two armchairs looked as if they had often been sat on. And then it was so big and the view was so wonderful, across a lawn planted with shrubs and palms and many flowers to a line of casuarinas through which the sea, now touched with crimson from the setting sun, gleamed.

Turning away from the windows she looked across the room at the wardrobe and on sudden impulse she went to it and slid back one of the doors. There were lightweight men's suits on hangers. She peered further in and saw rows of shirts. Closing the first door she slid open another and saw cotton slacks and even jeans hanging up. On the floor there were shoes.

She closed the door carefully and went back to her luggage to take out the sandals she intended to wear. She wasn't in a guestroom. She was in a room that was used regularly by a man and the only man she knew who lived in this house on a regular basis besides Tom Barlow was Kit Barlow. Sherri had shown her to this room because Sherri assumed she and Kit were still having an affair and still lived together when they could.

By the time she was ready to go downstairs the sun had almost set and the house was filled with rosy light and purple shadows. There was no sound of anyone being about so she made her way to the only room she knew, the big, long lounge

with the windows opening on to a terrace. Two
table lamps were lit shedding a golden glow.

There was a movement at the middle window. A
man stepped into the room. He paused when he
saw her. Across the room their eyes met and held.
It seemed to Stella that she had come full circle.
The only difference was that there were no groups
of laughing, talking people between them. For a
whole minute they stood staring at each other
warily. Then Kit moved, came towards her.

'Tom and Sherri have gone out,' he said coolly.
'We're to have dinner here, unless you'd like to go
somewhere else.'

'No, oh, no.' She was suddenly nervous. He was
looking at her so intently. 'Here will be fine ...
unless you'd like to go somewhere else.'

A slight smile curled his lips.'

'I usually eat here,' he drawled. 'I'll just go up
and shower and change, get rid of some of the salt.
See you in a few minutes.'

They dined in a small dining-room which also
opened on to the long terrace and from which
there was a view of the garden and the sea beyond.
Light faded while they ate and the long, dark,
tropical night set in. Outside, cicadas chirped.
Inside, silverware tinkled against china. They were
waited on by a small, silent Vietnamese, the
husband, Kit told Stella, to the cook-housekeeper
who was also from Vietnam. 'They are employed
by my mother who owns this house,' he added.

'Where is she now?' Stella asked.

'In England. She always goes there at this time
of the year. She gets homesick for April showers
and May blossom.'

'Don't you live here, then?'

'Only for part of the year. Most of the time now

I live in Charleston. I'll be flying back there day after tomorrow to keep an eye on things while Tom is having his vacation.'

They talked, but like strangers, unlike that first time they had met, thought Stella sadly, toying with her dessert, finding the tropical fruit cup suddenly tasteless. Then, there had been nothing between them. Both of them had been fresh, open to new adventures, their minds meeting and clicking instantly. Now experience and a certain amount of pride shut them off from each other.

'If you don't want the rest of your dessert I suggest we leave the table and go out on the terrace,' Kit's voice was dry and she looked across at him. He was watching her, a twist at the corner of his mouth.

She laid her linen table napkin beside her dish and stood up. The Vietnamese appeared silently. Kit gave him some instructions and he departed. Stella wandered away from the table outside. The warm air caressed her bare skin. From the shore came the sibilance of waves washing along the sand. She leaned against the stone balustrade and looked out at the shadowed garden.

'I hope you like cognac,' said Kit coming over to her. She turned to him and he offered her a goblet in which the tawny liqueur swayed. She took it from him. In the glow from the lanterns which lit the terrace only half his face was illuminated. The other half was in shadow. But she could see enough. She could see that the twist was still there marring the shapeliness of his lips.

'I'd give you a toast only I don't know what the hell to toast to,' he said bitterly. 'So I'll just say, here's to us.'

'Here's to us,' she repeated faintly. The glasses

clinked. They tipped them to their mouths. There was silence. From inside the room came the clink of dishes as they were removed from the table.

'Let's go and sit down,' said Kit and turning, walked along the terrace to some cushioned chairs which were set outside the windows of the big lounge. Slowly, Stella followed, sat down and put her glass down on the table. There was enough cognac in it to make her drunk, she thought with amusement, especially after the wine she had had at dinner.

'Remember the first time you came to this house?' Kit asked abruptly.

'Yes, I do. It's a lovely house.'

'I was going to ask you to come and stay here for a few days when we returned to Nassau at the end of our cruise together three and a half years ago.'

Stella said nothing. She found she was holding her breath and waiting, waiting for him to say more, afraid to speak herself in case she said something wrong but when the silence continued longer than she had expected she realised he was expecting her to make some comment. She sipped some more brandy and looked across at him. There wasn't so much light on that part of the terrace and his face was a mystery again.

'If you had asked me to stay I would have stayed,' she murmured. Sitting there looking out at the darkened garden across which once they had walked hand in hand to the beach memories were coming thick and fast, of all their times together and, in particular, of the moments on *Siren* at Nassau when he hadn't asked her to stay. Raising her head she looked across at him again and said more loudly, almost accusingly, 'Oh, why didn't you ask me? Why didn't you? Why did you let me leave you?'

He raised his head too, sharply and she caught the glint of light in his eyes.

'I let you leave?' he repeated, his voice rising a little. 'If I remember rightly you wanted very much to leave. You were damned feisty when I came back to the boat to ask you. You'd changed in a few minutes. You'd become a stiff and starchy feminist with only one thing in view. A career.' She heard the sneer in his voice. 'Who was I to come between a woman and her career? And I didn't want to. It's never suited me to play second fiddle either to another man or to a career.' He lifted his glass and drank more brandy. 'You left because you wanted to, Stella, not because I let you,' he added.

'I left because I believed you were going to marry Sherri,' she replied steadily.

The silence which followed her statement simmered with all kinds of unspoken expletives yet when he spoke his voice was very quiet, silken with menace.

'Say that again,' he said.

'I . . . I saw and heard Sherri when she came along the dock to welcome you. I saw the way she greeted you. She kissed and hugged you as if . . . as if she were very fond of you.'

'She is fond of me and I of her, but her hugging and kissing didn't mean any more than that,' he interrupted her coldly.

'And she said: "Now we can be married. Now we can set the date." So it was easy for me to believe that you had returned to marry her.'

His glass crashed down on the table with such force she thought it would shatter into smithereens.

'You believed that Sherri and I . . .' he began and broke off to draw in his breath hissingly. He leaned across the table threateningly. 'Then why the hell didn't you say so at the time?' he demanded harshly.

'I was too angry. And disappointed.'

'Disappointed?'

'In you. I believed the same of you as you believed of me on Sanada. I believed you to be a liar and a cheat; that you had taken me sailing with you as . . . as a last amorous fling before you settled down to married life.' Her voice faltered a little, then all that disappointment which she had felt and had smothered for years burst out, 'Oh you've no idea how hurt I was,' she cried. 'How unhappy, to think that you had used me in that way.'

There was another silence then the legs of his chair scraped on the stone floor of the terrace. He stood up paced over to the balustrade and stood there looking out at the garden for a few moments before turning and pacing back to stand in front of her, hands in the pockets of the well-cut, navy blue cotton twill trousers he was wearing.

'So you left without giving me a chance to put you right,' he said in a savage undertone, as he leaned towards her. 'My God, that was arrogant of you, Stella, arrogant and foolish.'

'I may have been foolish but never arrogant,' she retorted, seared by his rebuke and glaring up at him. 'I . . . I was too hurt to be that.'

'And I suppose it never occurred to you that I could be hurt too, because after all we had done together, after all we had *been* to each other, all you wanted was to leave me and . . .'

'But we'd made no commitment to each other,' she burst out defensively. 'You said right from the start that I was to feel free to leave when I wanted, that it would be over when we returned to Nassau because there was something else you had to do. How was I to know you would ask me to stay on?'

'When we started out I had no idea how deeply and emotionally involved I was going to become with you, no idea at all,' he said softly, taking his hands from his pockets. He placed them on her shoulders and lifted her to her feet. 'I'd no idea I was going to fall in love with you, Stella.'

'Love,' she whispered. 'Did you say love?'

'I did. I missed you damnably when you'd gone.' His hands slid down her bare arms, slowly and caressingly. Her skin tingled to that warm touch.

'Oh, I missed you too. Damnably,' she admitted.

'Then why didn't you write to me?' He was holding her hands now in his and squeezed them brutally between his as if he wanted to punish her in some way. 'I asked you to.'

'I didn't because I thought you were married to Sherri. Anyway, what about you? If you missed me so much why didn't you write to me?' she challenged him.

'What was the point? I believed you were married to your career,' he retorted bitterly.

'Then why did you go to Sanada?'

'A good question,' he mocked, 'I went out of curiosity to find out if the career was satisfactory and all you had hoped it would be. And I guess I wanted to test myself, find out if I was cured of my love for you.'

'And were you?' She asked the question hesitantly. Her hands still held in his grasp, she looked up at him trying to read his expression.

'No.'

'Does that mean . . .' she began breathlessly and couldn't go on.

'It means this,' he murmured stepping closer to her dropping her hands and putting his arms around her, drawing her against him. His cheek against her hair he went on in a whisper, 'It means I still want you, Stella, but only on my terms, only if you'll stay and live with me where I want to live, only if you'll give up that career of yours. I'm not sharing you with it. Or with any professor of archaeology.'

'I had no idea you could be so possessive, so demanding,' she teased, putting her hands against his chest pushing him away a little so that she could look up at his shadowed face.

'Neither had I until I saw you with Haines, saw him kiss you, heard him order you about.' His arms tightened about her threatening to cut off her breath. 'God, I was jealous. I could have throttled him quite cheerfully and you too.'

'Oh, Kit, if you knew how much I've wanted to hear you say something like that,' she said, half laughing at herself but inwardly amazed at how much his display of masterful jealously excited and pleased her. He was the lover she needed, a man who could sweep her off her feet, invade and take over her passionate heart. 'I've loved you for so long,' she admitted at last.

'You have?' He seemed surprised.

'For years. But I could never be sure of you. You've always enjoyed your freedom so much.'

'I've found out the hard way that freedom isn't too great if there is no one to share the enjoyment with,' he drawled drily.

'And then you don't seem to want to be committed to anyone.'

'You want commitment?' he asked gruffly.

'Only if you want to make it,' she replied softly.

'I want to make it to you but only to you.' He framed her face with his hands. 'How about this for starters?'

His lips sought hers. Warm and hard they pressed gently at first, moving subtly against sensitive skin, coaxing the response that rushed up from the depths of her being. The flame of desire his touch always lit in her flared up within her, naked and unashamed, because he was the man she loved, the only man she had ever loved and to him she would willingly give her body and soul.

Closely they clung to each other unaware of the velvety romantic darkness of the tropical night around them, of the scents of blossoms, the gleam of moonlight, the distant sigh of the sea, aware only of the awakening of sensations that only each of them could arouse in the other: the delicious tingle of delicate nerve endings beneath the skin, the taste of passion on their tongues, the noontime heat of it throbbing along their veins, blazing into their minds.

'How was that?' asked Kit, thickly and breathlessly, when he lifted his mouth from hers.

'Very good for starters,' she whispered shakily, still clinging to him because she seemed to have lost all her strength and could no longer stand without his support. 'But I want more, much more. I want it to go on for ever and to be always available.'

'Then you will have to make some commitment too,' he said. 'Will you stay and live with me? Will you give up all idea of going back to England to finish that doctorate? Will you fly with me to Charleston? We could be married there as soon as we can get a licence.'

'But you haven't proposed to me,' she reminded him, laughing again.

'So I'm proposing now. Will you marry me, Stella?'

'But I thought—you've always said you didn't want to marry anyone.'

'I've said a lot of damn fool things in my time,' he admitted. 'But if marrying you is the only way I can hold on to you I'm prepared to do it.' He jerked her roughly against him, his arms going around her tightly again and whispered into her hair, 'If you don't agree to marry me I won't sleep with you tonight or any other night. If you don't agree it finishes the affair, once and for all. I'll move your bags out of my room and you can find another place to sleep.'

'Oh, it is your room. I guessed it was.' She pulled away from him. 'But why was my luggage put in it?'

'I guess because it was addressed to me by Juan and not to you. Shall I move it out? Would you prefer another room?'

He stepped back from her and without his arms around her, without his warmth enclosing her she felt chilled and almost rejected. The moment of commitment for her had come, she realised. Leaving Brian and following Kit to tell him she wasn't going to marry Brian, making love with Kit, giving him the freedom of her body, was not enough for him. He wanted more too. He wanted her to make a much harder choice, the choice between a career and becoming his wife. Could she do it? Could she give up all she had struggled for, all she had studied for? Or could she give him up? Standing there before him she experienced a sudden flash of insight into a future life without him. It would be lonely, a grey desolate waste without his companionship, without his love. She didn't want such a life that would be no life at all. She couldn't leave him again, and she was sure that, somehow, she would be able to take up the threads of her career along the way.

'No, don't move them out,' she said, stepping close to him and lifting her arms about his neck. 'You see I would like to marry you. I want to sleep with you tonight and every night. Oh, Kit, put your arms around me and don't ever let me leave you again. Hold me, keep me for ever.'

For a brief and painfully tantalising moment she thought he wasn't going to respond to her commitment, her absolute surrender because he didn't move. He didn't sweep her into his arms and kiss her. He just stood still and silent. Then he said with a touch of mockery, 'You know, I don't really go for all this romantic tropical darkness, this standing about on terraces in the moonlight. I'd like to take you to a place where I can see you and make love to you properly. Let's go to bed.'

'But your brother and Sherri? Won't they be back soon? Won't they wonder where we are?' she asked as taking her hand he began to rush her across the big room where they had first met.

'They've gone aboard *Dolphin*. They decided to set off on their cruise tonight. We have the whole house to ourselves. You know I'm beginning to think Sherri set us up, showing you into my room. I wonder how she knew I wanted you to stay the night with me?'

'She must have guessed when I told her that I once believed you and she were going to be married the first time I saw her,' she said as he opened the door of the big bedroom. Light already

glowed softly from the bedside lamps and the
bedclothes had been turned down. 'Oh, what a
fool I was not to say anything to you about her
then,' she whispered, turning to him.

'We were both fools,' he murmured generously,
closing in on her. He raised a hand and stroked
her hair back from her face. 'But you are the most
beautiful fool I know,' he added, 'and I'm glad
you're going to marry me.'

There was a sultry darkness in his glance that
made her nerves tingle. Against her throat his
fingers stroked and slid down the V of the bodice
of her dress coming to rest provocatively at the
cleft between her breasts.

'All that time apart from each other. All that
time I believed you were married to Sherri. Time
wasted,' she whispered, swaying towards him.

'It wasn't wasted. Could be we both needed that
time apart to find out that we love each other and
need to be together. Could be we both had to learn
that commitment is not such a bad thing after all,
that love isn't love unless there is commitment,' he
said, serious for a few moments.

'But suppose you hadn't come to Sanada
instead of Jack Cowan? Supposing we hadn't met
again? Oh, Kit, it doesn't bear thinking about.'

'Then don't think about it, honey,' he suggested,
his voice soft and deep. 'Think about how I did
come when I knew you would be there. I was
working on how to find you again. I had a few
other leads.' He paused then said roughly, 'Is there
no easy way of taking this dress off you? Am I
going to have to rip it off?'

She laughed and danced away from him
towards the bed where she lifted the dress over her
head and tossed it aside. He came up behind her,

Merry Christmas
one and all.

CHANCES ARE
Barbara Delinsky

THE GIFT OF HAPPINESS
Amanda Carpenter

ONE ON ONE
Jenna Lee Joyce

HAWK'S PREY
Carole Mortimer

AN IMPRACTICAL PASSION
Vicki Lewis Thompson

TWO WEEKS TO REMEMBER
Betty Neels

A WEEK FROM FRIDAY
Georgia Bockoven

YESTERDAY'S MIRROR
Sophie Weston

More choice for the Christmas stocking. Two special reading packs from Mills & Boon. Adding more than a touch of romance to the festive season.

AVAILABLE: OCTOBER, 1986   PACK PRICE: £4.80

Mills & Boon